Invisible Death

E. Alan Fleischauer

FIRST EDITION, MAY 2023

Copyright 2023 by E. Alan Fleischauer

All rights reserved.
Published and printed in the United States of America.

This is a work of fiction. Names, characters, places, and incidents either are the product of the author's imagination or are used fictitiously. Any resemblance to actual persons, living or dead, events, or locales is strictly coincidental.

Yellow "1970 Jaguar XKE" image by dave_7
Red "1970 Jaguar XKE" image by Greg Gjerdingen
from Willmar, MN USA

Invisible Death

Dedication

I dedicate this book, my thirteenth, to my wife Paula Dawn Fleischauer. She is the love of my life, and my princess—in fact, I gave her a golden locket the says just that. Paula has a smile that lights up a room and a delightful giggle, and I could not go through life without her by my side. Thankfully, I don't need to. She is a retired nurse and looks after me diligently, especially since my heart events. So, Paula: I love you forever.

Prologue

JAKE SILVER WAS DRESSED in a spiffy black tuxedo, waiting impatiently at the altar. The church was packed with friends dressed to the nines, all there for Jake and Beth Ann's wedding. But Beth Ann wasn't there. Jake finished a brief conversation with Pastor Dawson and strode toward the back of the church, nodding at the guests, who were as perplexed and impatient as Jake was. At the back of the cathedral, Jake approached his good friend Omar Carter. "Where the heck is she?" Jake inquired.

Omar shook his head. "This isn't like her at all. I hope she's OK."

Jake pushed the church door open and ventured out onto the steps. It was a perfect June day, with brilliant blue skies and nary a cloud. Perfect ... but for the missing bride. Omar Jake on the steps and nodded at a black Lincoln Town Car that had pulled up in front of the church. "Maybe that's her."

The passenger door opened and a black-clad man emerged quickly. He appeared to be Asian and was short with incredibly wide shoulders. The man hurried up the steps with an envelope in his hand and bowed slightly as he handed the envelope to Jake. His face revealed no expression and he said nothing. Then he spun on his heel and hurried back to the car, slamming the door behind him with a loud thud. The Lincoln then pulled away from the curb with screeching tires.

Jake furrowed his brow. "What the hell was that?"

"I don't know," replied Omar. "Open the letter."

Jake tore the envelope open and pulled out a single sheet.

Dear Mr. Jake Silver,

Please be advised that your future bride, Ms. Beth Ann Noble, is alive and well. It's not my intention to harm her in any way, as long as you consent to help us with a few assignments that require your unique skill. As you read this, Ms. Noble is on her way to North Korea, where she'll be treated like a princess. I look forward to making her acquaintance and to having you comply with my future requests.

Sincerely,

Kim Jong-un

As Jake read the letter, his eyes opened wide, and he drew in a sharp breath. "What the fuck!" he said as he handed the letter to Omar. "This can't be happening!" he exclaimed.

But it was.

1

Dr. Treavor Storm was having breakfast in the cafeteria of Homeland Security with agent Chip Andrews. Chip was chuckling about their meeting the day before with POTUS-- the president of the United States.

"You know, Treavor, that's the first time I've ever been in the Oval Office," Chip said. "It really isn't all that special. It looked a little outdated ... you know, like Richard Nixon would have been happy with it."

Treavor grunted. "From what I've heard, I don't think Tricky Dick was ever happy about anything."

Chip swallowed his egg and pointed his index finger at the chair where Dr. Treavor Storm was sitting. "You got me there," he said.

A young woman paused as she walked past the table. "Chip, are you talking to yourself again? You know, you really need to get a life."

Treavor laughed, and the woman paused, then moved along with a perplexed expression.

"I guess not everyone knows that the invisible Dr. Treavor Storm, is in the building," Chip said. "So anyway, how did you like meeting the president?"

Treavor laughed softly. "I thought he was going to faint when he shook my hand." "I guess it was his first time meeting an invisible man."

"What did you expect? He's a freakin' politician. Stealing lollipops from babies is more up his alley. But he did present you with the Presidential Medal of Freedom."

Treavor toyed with the medal. "You know, I still feel like I shouldn't have accepted it. I killed two men on that flight."

"That's nonsense, and you know it. You saved a planeload of people and everyone in the new World Trade Center."

Treavor shrugged as Chip's cell phone chimed. "It's Da Boss," Chip said as he took the call.

"Yes, sir, good morning to you. Absolutely. He's sitting right across from me and is just finishing a half pound of bacon. For an invisible dude, he sure can pack it away. Yes sir, I'll tell him."

Chip turned to where Treavor was sitting. "Da Boss says if you don't eat, you die, so finish eating. When you're done, he may have a new mission for you."

Treavor popped the last bit of bacon into his mouth. "Sure, why not? Now that I'm an employee of HS, I might as well earn my pay ... as long as I don't have to kill anyone else."

❖❖❖❖❖

Chip and Treavor walked into Da Boss's office. He was dressed in a tan suit with light blue vertical stripes; a powder-blue dress shirt; and a multicolored Jerry Garcia necktie. His desk was completely bare but for his phone. Homeland Security Agent Ted Janick and a middle-aged man were sitting in guest chairs.

Da Boss gestured at two of the empty seats and said, "Chip, Treavor, please sit down." He glanced at his guests. "I'd like to introduce you to HS Agents Ted Janick and Jake Silver."

Chip leaned over with a quick smile and shook Jake's hand. "I've heard quite a bit about you from Ted. Nice to finally meet you."

Jake flashed a quick smile. "Yeah, same here."

Treavor spoke up. "Mr. Silver, if you stretch out your hand, I'll shake it. I'm Dr. Treavor Storm."

Jake grunted softly. "Da Boss said you were invisible, but I thought he was bullshitting me."

Treavor gripped Jake's hand. "Nope, I'm really invisible, whether I like it or not."

"Well, nice to meet you. This is a first for me, meeting an invisible dude."

"Yeah, not a lot of us around."

"On the other hand, how would we know?" Jake asked.

Treavor laughed softly. "That's true."

Da Boss interjected. "Dr. Storm, the reason I wanted you to meet Mr. Silver is that he has a special skill as well. Jake has the ability to point at things--animals and people--and say, 'Just die,' and they do—immediately."

Treavor took a quick breath. "I heard about that from Chip when I first met him, but I thought it was a bit farfetched."

Jake snorted. "Yeah, tell me about it. Truthfully, it sucks."

Da Boss continued. "Be that as it may, both of you have served your country admirably with your special gifts, and I'm thinking of teaming you up. Jake has a dilemma on his hands, and Treavor, you may be able to help him and HS as well."

Treavor studied Jake. It was obvious that he was upset. His eyes were flat, and he seemed to be in a sullen funk. "Hmm ... OK, tell me about it."

Jake explained about the aborted wedding and the uninvited visitor. "So I opened the letter and it's from North Korean dictator Kim Jong-un, expressing an interest in utilizing my killing ability."

Da Boss interrupted. "To make a long story short, Jake assisted the president with a mission in Korea and Russia that was supported by Kim Jong-un. He's aware of Jake's special skill, and now he wants to use him for his own purposes. To that end, he has kidnapped Jake's fiancée."

Treavor moaned and eyed Jake Silver again. "Man, I'm sorry. That's horrific," he said.

"Yeah, it is," replied Jake. "I'm not sure what he wants me to do, but it can't be good."

Treavor touched Jake on the arm. "I'm sure it isn't. So, how can I help?"

Jake shook his head. "I have no idea."

Da Boss cleared his throat. "We haven't figured all of it out yet, Dr. Storm, but we will. Now that you're an HS agent, this is exactly the kind of thing we signed you up for. We need to see what Kim Jong-un has in mind, then we'll make a decision. We may require your special skills."

Treavor pursed his invisible lips and nodded. "I'll absolutely do whatever I can to help Mr. Silver. Remember, though, I will not kill anyone. I still have nightmares about the last time."

Jake snorted loudly. "Leave the killing to me. That's what I do best," he said somberly.

No one laughed.

❖❖❖❖❖

The next day, Jake Silver received an email from North Korea from a representative of Kim Jong-un. Jake was instructed to kill South Korea's former president, Park Geun-hye. She had been impeached on charges of influence peddling, corruption, and abuse of power. She was sentenced to 25 years in prison, but received a pardon from South Korean President Yoon Suk Yeol. While in office, she had vowed to overthrow Kim Jong-un, and now he wanted revenge.

The HS crew met in Da Boss's office that afternoon to discuss the situation. Chip Andrews turned to Jake Silver and said, "Well, that didn't take long."

"I'll say. Now what do I do? If I don't follow through, they may well kill Beth Ann, and I can't let that happen."

Da Boss nodded. "Yes, that's quite possible because Kim Jong-un appears to have no compunction about killing people. In fact, I think he rather enjoys it."

"Goddammit! I'll do what he wants if that what it takes to keep Beth Ann alive!" Jake replied.

Da Boss grunted, stood up, and went to the window. The day was warm for that time of year, partly cloudy with a nice breeze.. He turned back toward the crew and looked directly at Jake. "Maybe we can do both,"

Chip grimaced. "What are you talking about?"

Da Boss sucked in a breath. "Well, the president has an excellent relationship with Yoon Suk Yeol, and Park Geun-hye is also indebted to him. Maybe she can be convinced to disappear for a while. Meanwhile, our governments can tell the press that she has died while we figure out how to rescue Beth Ann."

Chip nodded. "That might work."

Jake shrugged and said nothing.

Da Boss sat back in his chair. "All right. Let's see if POTUS will cooperate."

❖❖❖❖❖

The US president approved the plan. The South Korean president was agreeable once the US president explained the situation to him, even revealing Jake Silver's "just die" powers. Late the next day, President Yoon Suk Yeol reported that Park Geun-hye was willing to play along, but with a few conditions. First, she wanted $1 million for her efforts. Second, she wanted her entire entourage to be put up at a resort of her choosing for a year. Finally, she wanted to meet Jake Silver in person.

Three days later, Jake, Treavor, Chip, and Ted boarded the HS plane, a Gulfstream G700, for Seoul. The flight attendants were introduced to Dr. Storm well after takeoff so that they would be unable to decide to skip this flight. As it turned out, they were enthralled to be flying with an invisible man, especially one who was so polite. Jake's special skill wasn't mentioned.

During the flight, Treavor and Jake talked about how they ended up with their afflictions. Treavor explained how he had gone out for his morning run in early January and slipped on the icy sidewalk in front of his home. Two hours later, he woke up covered with snow and ice, nearly frozen to death. He then crawled into his house, into the shower, then out and up to the fog-covered mirror. When he wiped off the mirror ... *poof!* He couldn't see himself. Then he explained to Jake about being able to see himself in a two-way mirror, then finally about his fiancée, Lizzy, calling off their marriage and hooking up with a surgeon.

Jake told Treavor about having a mild stroke, waking up, pointing at things and people, and whenever he said "Just die," they did. His mother taught him to say that when he drove at an early age, as opposed to giving someone the finger. "Just die," that is. And now, he had the power—or curse.

As they rode together, the two unique men began to form a bond. Peas in two different pods with unique talents.

❖❖❖❖❖

While Treavor and Jake were winging it to Seoul, Travis Storm, Treavor's autistic younger brother, was staying at Treavor's house in South Minneapolis. He was house-sitting, enjoying not having to live with his parents.

Travis was just finishing up a spicy chicken Chick-fil-A sandwich when the doorbell rang. He stood up, sandwich in hand, and scooted to the door. He opened the door as he took a hefty bite, and his head snapped back. There stood a gorgeous blond woman on the front porch with a microphone in her hand. She had high cheekbones, a nose that wasn't her own, and just a bit too much makeup on her cat-like face. She wore tan slacks, a bright-yellow blouse, a black blazer, and alligator shoes with four-inch heels. A very scruffy man stood off to one side holding a large TV camera.

"Is this Dr. Treavor Storm's home?" she asked as she pushed the microphone in Travis' face.

Travis swallowed. "Um ... yeah."

"Is he at home now?"

"Um ... no, he's traveling."

"Really? And who are you, sir?"

Travis wiped his mouth with the back of his hand, then licked off a spot of stray mayonnaise. "I'm his brother Travis."

"I understand that Dr. Storm is invisible. Is that correct?"

"Where did you hear that?"

"From a reliable source. A police officer who escorted him home while he was driving."

"Hmm ... well, yeah. I guess it's not a secret if the police know about it. Yes, he's invisible,"

"Oh my God, have you seen him?"

Travis laughed. "Don't be a dope. He's invisible."

The woman frowned. "You know what I meant."

Travis shook his head. "You know, I really don't think I should be talking to you, and I need you to go. You have a nice evening." Then he closed the door with a thud.

Hmm ... that was unexpected. Gosh, I hope I don't get Treavor in trouble. Oh well, he's meeting the president of the United States to get a medal, so hell, even the president knows Treavor is invisible.

❖❖❖❖❖

After landing in Seoul, the four HS agents got into a limo that took them to a hotel in a tower in Songpa-Gu. The building rivaled the new World Trade Center in New York City, with the hotel taking up floors 76 to 101.

Fortunately, all the reception clerks spoke English. They quickly checked in and were ushered to their rooms by a bellhop who also spoke nearly perfect English. Jake Silver got the presidential suite. The rest of the group were given standard rooms.

The crew gathered in Jake's suite and ordered room service, supplemented by the minibar. Treavor had a Coke, Jake a gin and tonic, Ted Janick a Scotch neat, and Chip a rum and Coke.

Chip sipped his cocktail and studied Ted. "Da Boss tells me that you were a highly decorated officer in the Coast Guard ... something about a hurricane."

Ted shrugged. "It was no big deal, a mountain made out of a molehill."

"That's not what Da Boss said."

Ted grunted from his massive chest. "Da Boss." He paused and sipped his Scotch. "You know, I don't even know his first name."

Chip stroked his chin. "Well, his last name is Redford. That's all I know."

Ted chuckled. "Maybe his first name is Robert Not that there's the slightest resemblance."

❖❖❖❖❖

The next day, they were whisked off to the Korean presidential residence. The limo driver escorted them into the reception room, where President Yoon Suk Yeol greeted them. Introductions were made, and he asked them to follow him into an outdoor area in the back where Park Geun-hye was seated. She was small, with short, black hair, a rounded chin, lovely complexion, and a "been there, done that" look on her face.

Park stood up with a glimmer of a smile on her full lips, then executed a bow at the waist. Introductions were made, and everyone sat in comfortable wicker chairs. Treavor stood away from the group, leaning against an ancient oak with a good view of Park. Naturally, he wasn't introduced.

Park turned to Jake and said, "I understand that your fiancée has been kidnapped by my old nemesis, Kim Jong-un. My condolences."

Jake nodded. "I'm grateful for your assistance."

"Well, from what I'm told, he's out to assassinate me, sooner or later."

"Yes, I would surmise so. He has enlisted my services ... because of a special skill."

Park leaned forward. "And what would that be?"

Ted spoke up. "Ma'am, Mr. Silver can simply point at things, say 'Just die,' and they do ... immediately."

Park jerked back. "I'm not sure I understand."

Jake considered Yoon Suk Yeol and pointed at the oak tree's branches, which were filled with ravens. "Sir, would you mind if I kill a raven?"

Yoon replied, "Please do. Kill them all. They're not welcome here, as they're a sign of death."

Jake stood up and pointed at the ravens, one at a time, then twiddled his fingers and said, "Just die." They dropped *en masse,* with one hitting Treavor on his shoulder.

Park flashed a dry smile. "My, my, that's impressive." She turned to look at Jake. "So, you could point at me, say 'Just die,' and I would be dead?"

"Yes, ma'am."

"Well, then I'd be happy to assist you. I'm certainly not ready to die, but I can certainly pretend to be dead."

Ted Janick stood up. "Perhaps we could have you lie down as if you're dead and we will snap a few photos."

Pictures were taken from several angles, including a number of close-ups of Park's face. They included a few of the dead crows scattered all around her, then one with Jake squatting down next to her with a stone-faced expression.

After the photo session, Park moved toward Jake and stretched out her hand. "Good luck recovering your future wife. I'll enjoy being dead for a while. Kim Jong-un isn't long for this world, from what I'm told. Meanwhile, I'll enjoy the beach, catch up on my reading, and spend your government's money on wonderful food. I looked up your Homeland Security budget online—52.2 billion dollars. I guess I should have asked for more than a million dollars."

.

2

RICHARD BEASLEY'S FATHER, may he rest in peace, was a jeweler. His son, nicknamed Dickie, had no patience for running a jewelry store, and as soon as his father was in the grave, he sold it and moved on to stealing jewels instead of selling them.

Dickie put the proceeds up his nose in the form of cocaine and recently graduated to methamphetamine. Now he was killing himself with the drug, and he really didn't give a shit. He had been in and out of rehab when his father was still around, and it didn't take. He lived for meth, and all he wanted was an endless supply and to die an early death. Life without the drug was no option.

Dickie watched Travis Storm being interviewed on TV, and the idea that Travis' brother was invisible intrigued him. An invisible man could be of use to him. In fact, he could make him rich beyond his wildest dreams. *Dr. Treavor Storm, with a little brother, Travis. Interesting. I need to do a little research.*

❖❖❖❖❖

South Korean President Yoon Suk Yeol, through intermediaries, announced that Park Geun-hye had disappeared and was feared dead. Jake emailed the staged photos of Park's body to Kim Jong-un's people. That afternoon, they all boarded the Gulfstream and headed back home. Treavor was nursing a bit of indigestion from the cabbage, and Jake was wondering how Beth Ann was being treated. Ted was curious about what Jake's new assignment from Kim Jong-un would be.

As it turned out, they didn't have to wait long before they all found out. The next assignment was to eliminate President Nguema of Equatorial Guinea. Apparently, the dictator had been an ally of North Korea, but the United States, in its everlasting search for cheap oil, had welcomed Nguema back into the fold, so to speak. A photo of Nguema and former President Obama, taken in the White House, set Kim Jong-un off on a murderous tirade.

Given that President Nguema had a long history of abuses--including his security forces' various murders, government-sanctioned kidnapping, systematic torture of prisoners, etc.--Homeland Security had no problem with killing him, as long as it was off the record and required minimal governmental support. Prime Minister Manuela Roka Botey, a moderate who would support the democratic way of life, would be his likely successor.

A plan was devised to have Jake and Treavor fly into the capital city of Malabo, which was on the island of Bioko on the rim of a sunken volcano. Jake was to pose as a recently hired executive from Exxon Mobil. The company had been apprised of the situation and, knowing better than to question Homeland Security, would answer any inquiries from Nguema's minions.

Soon, the gang of four—Jake, Treavor, Ted, and Chip—were winging their way to Africa. Same plane, same pilots, same flight attendants.

On the long trip, Jake filled Treavor in on the situation in North Korea. There was intelligence that Kim Jong-un was thinking of giving up his nuclear weapons program, but that a few young and untouchable generals stood in his way. Jake had been enlisted to do kill them at a beach resort in Russia. While he did succeed, he did it rather messily, to the chagrin of Kim. He thought that maybe the kidnapping of Beth Ann was, in part, his punishment for that screw-up.

Treavor talked about his last assignment, a spur-of-the-moment mission to intercept hijackers who had commandeered a Delta flight, ostensibly for a huge ransom. But that was a ruse, as the real plan was to crash the plane into the new World Trade Center. Treavor had thwarted the plan by killing the mastermind in the nick of time.

Afterward, they passed the time talking about their personal lives. Treavor had an older brother, Thomas, who was a Lutheran minister, and one younger, Travis, who was on the autism spectrum. His only sister, Tanya, was a top-level member of the Bureau of Criminal Apprehension (BCA).

Jake talked about Beth Ann and how he killed her pedophilic father, something for which she was actually quite grateful. He also discussed his friend Omar Carter, a former Green Bay Packer football player. Omar was set to be his best man at Jake's wedding to Beth Ann, and he was bound and determined to help Jake rescue her any way he could. As the hours passed, the two men with unique skills were beginning to form a solid friendship, eager to help each other.

Finally, the plane landed in Equatorial Guinea. Everyone was jet-lagged but keyed up for the assignment. They had arranged for a limousine to take them to their hotel, the Sofitel Malabo Sipopo Le Golf, right on the ocean. From there, they would be picked up the next day for a ferry ride to the island of Bioko. Fun. The men spent the evening in their rooms, ordering room service and recuperating after the long flight.

The next morning, a black SUV picked them up in front of the hotel and took them to the ferry. The short passage through the bay was uneventful, and the day was moderately warm with a stiff breeze.

They arrived at an interesting building, a few stories tall, situated on the edge of the ocean and shaped like a humongous palm tree. The driver parked the car in front and escorted the men up to the top floor. They were led to a conference room with a marvelous view of the ocean. The driver motioned for them to sit, then closed the door and locked it.

An hour later the door opened and four men armed with nasty-looking sidearms entered, accompanied by Vice President Teodorin Nguema Obiang Mangue, the son of Nguema. He didn't look happy. He sat at the head of the table and glared at the HS agents as the four armed men each went to a corner, guns drawn. "So, gentlemen, which of you is Jake Silver?" he inquired.

Jake nodded and raised a finger. "That would be me."

"I understand you're here to assassinate my father."

Jake's head snapped back. "Um ... no, sir. Not at all."

"Ah, but you are. You see, we have sources in Irving, Texas, and we have it on good authority that you are, indeed, tasked with this." He looked at Chip and Ted. "What we don't understand is why you're being accompanied by two members of the United States Homeland Security forces."

Chip started to say something, but Teodorin waved him off. "It makes no difference. You two will be escorted back to your jet, and you are to leave the country, never to return." Then he looked at Jake. "You, on the other hand, will be our guest and take advantage of our hospitality," he said with a nasty smirk.

Chip and Ted were escorted out of the room and Jake sat motionless, wondering what he should do. He could point at Teodorin just and say "Just die," but he'd never have time to take out the four gunmen before he was full of bullets.

He then heard a faint whisper in his left ear. "Hang in there, Jake. We'll get out of this. I'll be right next to you."

Teodorin leaned forward. "You see, Mr. Silver, we don't know why a retired financial adviser is tasked with assassinating my father, but we will find out, as we are experts in torture. If there was a gold medal for torture, my father would have won it. I would only take the silver medal, but I am a quick study, as you are about to learn."

Jake was handcuffed behind his back and led downstairs to another black SUV. From there, he was taken back to the ferry and the mainland, followed by a quick trip to a four-story brick building that poked out of the terrain like a sore thumb.

Jake was thrown into a battered elevator that smelled of urine and puke, then taken down to a basement where a long line of cells awaited him. Most of the cells were occupied by listless men who had seen better days. Jake shuddered involuntarily, hoping that Treavor Storm was nearby.

A guard opened an cell and pushed Jake inside, then he shoved his handgun into the back of Jake's head. "Stand still," he commanded as another henchman removed the handcuffs. When Jake turned around, he was whacked in the forehead with the butt of a pistol. His eyes rolled back, and he stepped backward. The guard laughed. "Welcome to your new home, asshole." Then he spun around and left, locking the cell. Jake moaned and sat down on a rock-hard mattress. Suddenly, a voice from outside the cell whispered, "Don't worry, Jake. I've got you covered. Hang in there!"

❖❖❖❖❖

Dickie Beasley had just printed out an old photo of Dr. Treavor Storm from the University of Minnesota website. He apparently was on a leave of absence. He leaned forward and examined the photo, nodding his approval. *Good-looking dude. Looks like a young George Clooney.*

He Googled Travis Storm and was soon looking at a picture of Travis from the St. David's Center website. After a little more browsing, he tracked down Travis' cell phone number and dialed it.

Travis answered on the third ring. "Hello?"

"Hello, is this Dr. Treavor Storm?" Dickie inquired.

"No, this is his brother Travis."

"Can you tell me how I would I reach Dr. Storm? This is the University of Minnesota, and we need to talk to him about his leave of absence."

"Well, sir, he's out of the country, and I have no idea when he'll be back."

Dickie paused. "OK, I appreciate it. You have a great day."

"You as well."

Out of the country. Damn. I wonder what that's all about?

❖❖❖❖❖

Jake stood up and moved to the cell bars. "Hey, Treavor, I'm glad you hung around."

Treavor chuckled quietly. "Well, I was thinking of leaving with Chip and Ted, and playing a round of golf at the hotel, but I decided against it."

"Yeah, very funny. These guys mean business, and we need to get me the hell out of here."

"You got that right. Let's wait awhile, then I'll do a little reconnoitering."

"OK, whatever," Jake said.

Twenty minutes later, the door at the far end of the cell block opened, and the two henchmen entered. One was chatting on Jake's cell phone, which he had confiscated earlier. "Yes, sir, we will take him to the torture room. See you in a bit."

Jake gave a start at the mention of torture, and he shook his head. *Nope, not going to happen.* He stepped back as the guard put the phone away and pulled out the keys to the cell. The other man raised his sidearm and pointed it at Jake. "Don't make me shoot you. We need to have some fun with you before we do that," he said with a sneer.

As t cell door swung open and the first man stepped in, Jake quickly pointed a finger at the man with the gun and said "Just die."

The man collapsed as if there were no gravity, dead as a doornail. The other man turned around with a puzzled look on his face. "What the fuck?" he said, totally confused.

Jake smiled. "Excuse me," he said, and tapped the henchman on the shoulder. When the man turned back toward him, Jake punched him in the nose. "How do you like that?" he yelled.

The man went for his gun.. Jake snorted and pointed. "Uh-uh, no can do. Why don't you...just die?" Which the man did, dead before he hit the floor.

Jake rubbed his stinging fist, took a deep breath, and glanced at the corpses. "Got what you deserved, assholes." He squatted down, retrieved the phone and handgun, and walked through the cell door. "Well, Dr. Storm, should we get the hell out of here?"

Treavor grunted. "Sounds good to me."

Jake headed toward the exit. As they passed the rest of the prisoners, one of the men called out to them, "Hey, let us out of here! Please!"

Jake stopped. "What do you think? Should we?"

"Absolutely," Treavor replied.

Jake turned and headed back to his cell, retrieved the keys, and proceeded to open every cell. Quiet cries of gratitude echoed throughout the cell block. One fellow with only one eye, the other having been gouged out, knelt down and took the second man's handgun and phone. Then he stood up, spit on him, then flashed a sparkling grin at Jake.

"You're right ... they are assholes!"

Just then, Teodorin entered the cell block and stopped in his tracks as he saw all the prisoners out of their cells. One of them immediately whacked him on the side of his head, and the rest quickly rushed forward and began to pummel him. He fell to his knees, covering his face, but it did little to stop the furious deluge of fists, elbows, and occasional kicks. Teodorin collapsed to the floor, and the beatings increased in intensity. Some of the men hooted and hollered for joy as they went about their business, punching and kicking, with some removing their shoes and striking the man with the heels.

"He is an evil man. We need to finish him," one man cried out. Jake and Treavor stood next to the one-eyed man and watched in awe.

Finally, Jake stepped forward and shouted, "Enough, step away." As soon as they did. Jake raised the pistol and shot

Teodorin in the forehead. He motioned to the ex-prisoners. "Get out of here. Go home to your families, stay hidden, and God bless."

As the men quickly dispersed, the one-eyed man turned to Jake and said, "Follow me."

"Just a minute," Jake replied. He squatted next to Teodorin's corpse. "Treavor, do you have your cell phone?"

"I do."

"Good. Take a couple of pictures of me with this asshole."

"Got it."

The one-eyed prisoner stood dumbfounded. "Who are you talking to?"

"Oh, that's my partner, Treavor. He's invisible," Jake said with a muted laugh.

The man shook his head and sighed. "This day is getting more and more interesting by the minute. But now, we need to hurry, so please follow me."

Outside, the man pulled out the cell phone as he hurried down the sidewalk. He talked for a moment, then disconnected the call. He stopped and waited for Jake to catch up, and they continued walking. "I called my brother to pick us up. He drives a taxi, and he'll meet us about a half mile from here." He paused. "By the way, my name is Miguel Santo. I understand your name is Jake?"

Yes, "Jake Silver. Nice to meet you."

"I don't know how you killed those men, but could you teach me?"

"No, and I wouldn't if I could. Believe me, it's not a skill you want."

Ten minutes later, a cab went passed them on the other side of the street, made a U-turn, and pulled up alongside the men. Miguel opened the passenger door, and Jake got in the back and slid over to the other side. Treavor entered behind him and closed the door. The driver, Sei Santo, turned and gaped at the closed door. "What the heck is going on here?"

Miguel laughed. "Just drive, Sei. This has been a most interesting day."

Sei grabbed Miguel's leg and gave it a squeeze. "It's so good to see you again, brother. We all thought you were dead."

Miguel nodded. "Sometimes I wished I was, but God had other plans for me. I think maybe we will start a revolution."

Sei grunted in agreement. "Sign me up!"

3

WHEN CHIP AND TED boarded the HS jet, the pilot and flight attendants were already on board. Twenty minutes later, they took off for Rwanda, a three-hour flight. The mission, in their minds, was a complete disaster, and Da Boss was notified just before they lifted off. It was his suggestion to land in Rwanda, as it was safe, and he had contacts in the country.

Meanwhile, Jake, Treavor, Miguel, and Sei pulled into Sei's modest home. Sei was a widower, and his children were no longer living with him, so the place was empty. The group headed in, and Miguel explained to Sei how he lost his eye. Teodorin Nguema had scooped it out with a brand-new, razor-sharp spoon, snickering as he did it. Miguel had been a reporter with the newspaper and had printed a not-so-favorable article about Teodorin getting tossed out of France for corruption and misdeeds. Apparently, Teodorin didn't see eye to eye with him, so he thought it appropriate to remove Miguel's eye.

The group sat in Sei's kitchen, and Sei busied himself with making a meal, as his brother was twenty-five pounds lighter than the last time he saw him. Jake explained how he had planned to assassinate President Nguema at the request of Kim Jong-un, using his "Just die" powers. Treavor explained briefly how he had become invisible. Miguel and Sei had a hard time believing either of them. On the other hand, Miguel had seen Jake in action, and Treavor was now sitting across from him, definitely invisible, sipping on a glass of water that disappeared, then reappeared randomly on the table.

When they were done with their brief explanation, Jake took out his phone and called Ted Janick. No answer. He looked at Treavor, sitting in his chair. "I think we're on our own. I'm not sure whether Ted and Chip are going to be able to help us."

"I think you're right, Jake. The question is, should we abort this assignment or continue to pursue daddy?

Miguel snorted at that. "Yeah, he says he's the father of us all. Just a benevolent daddy."

Sei set a few platters of food on the table. "Dig in, men. You never know when you may eat again."

As they ate, Sei said, "Jake, will be hunted. Nguema won't rest until he captures you and makes you pay. Understand, he's one of the wealthiest men in the world and has incredible resources. Unless he's stopped, he will find you and end you as painfully as possible."

Miguel grunted. "You can say that again. If I were you, I would just kill him first. Otherwise, your days are numbered."

Treavor spoke up. "Jake, I've been thinking that there is sure to be a state funeral. That may be your best opportunity to take Nguema out."

Jake sighed. "But how am I going to get near him? I'll be spotted the moment I show up." His eyes widened as an idea came to him. "But Treavor, you can't be spotted at all. I know that you hate to kill, but perhaps you could make an exception for me?"

It was Treavor's turn to sigh. "I just can't do that, Jake. I still have nightmares about the two men I killed on the plane, and I'm determined never to do it again."

Jake slumped in his chair. "I get it, I guess, but that makes me a dead man walking."

The men all sat silent as a sense of doom filled the room. Then Treavor spoke up.

"Wait, Jake. I just thought of a different solution." He picked up his water glass, and it disappeared. "You see, Jake, if I'm holding something—or someone—then they're invisible, too. So I could carry you into the funeral, and you could end Nguema without being seen. No one would be the wiser."

Jake furrowed his brow. "Are you sure that will work?"

"Yes, I've done it before. We could disguise you, then as we get near, I'll put you up on my shoulders in a fireman's carry and head in. You kill Nguema, and we get the heck out of there. Do you have a better idea? If so, I'm all ears."

Jake inhaled deeply. "No, I guess I don't. Why don't we try it out now?"

"Sure, why not?"

As Treavor picked him up, Jake vanished Miguel and Sei watched in amazement. Sei looked at Miguel and muttered, "Freakin' crazy Americans."

❖❖❖❖❖

It was three long days later when the four men piled into a borrowed car and headed toward Malabo Cemetery. They arrived while the church service for Teodorin was being held at the majestic, twin-steepled St. Elizabeth's Cathedral and waited at the cemetery, since Treavor didn't want to commit a sacrilege by assassinating President Nguema in a church. Also, at the cemetery Nguema would be an easier target.

Sei and Miguel dropped Jake and Treavor off at the far end of the cemetery and parked a few blocks away, out of sight. As they waited, Treavor asked Jake a question that had been on his mind.

"Say, Jake, I'm a bit curious. How do you feel about using your 'Just die' power? Do you regret killing anyone?"

Jake sighed. "Yes and no. I certainly don't do it indiscriminately. I do regret killing the first man, but I didn't know I had the power then. And the second man on the bike path behind my home was completely innocent. I would take those back if I could. But the rest ... no, they needed to die. Even Beth Ann's father."

Treavor shook his head. "I don't know how you do it. I certainly couldn't."

Jake laughed. "Well, I guess that's why God made you invisible. Different strokes for different folks, right?"

Jake looked up and saw a black hearse entering the cemetery, followed by a line of cars. The procession turned and headed toward a fresh grave where chairs were set up in a semicircle. The cars stopped and the occupants disembarked. Nguema emerged, looking resigned and determined. Then the back of the hearse was opened and the casket removed.

They walked to the side of the grave and sat in the weathered chairs. Nguema sat next to Constance Mangue, his wife. She was weeping, dabbing her eyes with a handkerchief. A small elderly man dressed in red moved up next to the casket and opened a Bible. He began speaking quietly.

Jake couldn't make out any words besides "God," "Jesus," and "Heaven." *Heaven? Really? Fat chance.*

Jake and Treavor waited until the cardinal finished and people began to stand up. Treavor looked at Jake. "Are you ready for this?"

"I am. Let's do it."

Treavor squatted and lifted Jake onto his shoulders, and Jake vanished from sight.

"How close do you need to be?" Treavor inquired.

"Fifty feet, to be safe, and I need a straight shot at him, no one in the way."

"Roger that. Here we go."

The day was excessively humid, with no hint of a breeze. The sun was a red ball floating above the horizon, hammering down through the thick air. The green leaves in the trees that dotted the cemetery appeared lifeless.

Mourners and bodyguards were gathered around Nguema and his wife at the gravesite. Unfortunately, there was no clean line of sight. Treavor circled around the group, weaving through gravestones, until Jake whispered, "Stop, this will do. Turn to the right a bit."

Jake sucked in a quick breath and called out, "Just die."

President Nguema toppled right into his son's grave. His wife gave a cry of surprise, and a bodyguard pulled a handgun and began shooting in the direction of Jake's voice. A bullet ricocheted off a gravestone two feet away from Jake and Treavor, and Treavor yelped as a few granite chips smacked him in the face. The shooter adjusted his aim, and a hot slug sped by Jake's forehead, too close for comfort.

Jake hissed, "Hey Treavor, now would be a good time to get the hell out of here!"

Treavor grunted, turned, and headed to where Miguel and Sei were waiting in the car. He ran for about fifty feet when he stumbled and fell, throwing Jake off his shoulders and onto the side of a gravestone. Jake moaned and grabbed his left wrist. "Son of a bitch. I think it's broken," he hollered.

Treavor quickly stood up as two more henchmen began to fire at the now-visible Jake. He flattened out and crawled behind a gravestone. The three men were running toward them, shouting while keeping up a steady barrage of fire. Treavor felt a slug whiz past his ear, then Jake leaned out just a bit from behind the gravestone and uttered, "Just die." All the guards dropped like empty sacks. Treavor moved toward Jake and grabbed his arm. "Come on, get up. Let's get out of here!" he exclaimed.

Running as fast as they could, they made it to the car and jumped into the back seat. Sei turned toward them as he put the car in gear and stepped on the gas. "We heard shots. What happened?"

Treavor responded, "I fell and threw Jake to the ground. He was visible then, so what you heard was the guards shooting at us."

"Oh, crap, that's not good."

"Well, Jake took care of them, so they won't be a problem, but it was too close for comfort."

Jake grunted. "No shit, Sherlock, and I think I fucking fractured my wrist."

"Better than getting shot."

Jake just moaned.

Sei drove to his house the long way, checking his rearview mirror to ensure that no one was tailing him. The homes in this residential area were mostly one-story bungalows, some painted bright yellow, pastel blue, or pink. The yards were manicured, with white and pink azalea shrubs, red hibiscus, and small blue wisteria trees dotting the landscape.

When Sei was satisfied that they weren't being followed, he pulled up into his short driveway. Everyone hopped out, and the men trooped up and into Sei's home, adrenaline still pumping. Sei set out glasses of Nolet's Silver Dry Gin. It was smooth, tasty, and packed a punch.

Jake wrapped his wrist with an ACE bandage and laid a bag of ice over it. A couple of ibuprofen helped to take the edge off the pain for now. He told Sei and Miguel what had happened at the funeral. "It was going pretty well until Mr.

Clumsy tripped." He chuckled softly as he looked at the couch where Treavor was seated.

"Horse hockey. They were already shooting at us," Treavor responded.

Jake took a long swig of his gin. "Yeah, but you really didn't need to slam me into a gravestone."

"Wuss," Treavor replied. Then he put his glass down. "So what happens now? Who will take over this country?"

Miguel leaned forward. "I don't know, but I would be very happy if the prime minister took charge."

Sei nodded his head emphatically. "Manuela is well-liked by the people. She's a moderate and was Nguema's peace offering to us. If she steps in, we will all be thankful."

"Well then, I hope she does," Jake replied. "In the meantime, pass me that bottle of gin. I'm getting drunk. Just for medicinal purposes, of course," he said with a grin.

❖❖❖❖❖

The next morning, the men woke up with the bright sun streaming through the windows. There wasn't a cloud in the sky, and it was shaping up to be a hot, steamy day.

Sei had coffee prepared and was working on breakfast—eggs, bacon, pork sausages, and cabbage fried with chopped onions. Jake was the last one to awaken, and he stumbled out of the bedroom, hung over and groaning. He sat at the kitchen table, and Sei poured him a cup of coffee.

"How are you feeling this morning, Mr. Jake?"

"Not so good."

"Have some food. It will help," Sei said.

Jake just groaned again and sipped the steaming coffee.

A television sat on the counter with the volume off when a video of the prime minister appeared on the screen. Sei grabbed the remote and turned on the sound.

"My fellow citizens," she said in Spanish, "I'm sad to report that our beloved president has passed. He was attending his son's funeral, and apparently, he had a heart attack. We're all in mourning, but life will go on. For now, I'm assuming control of the government, and we will have a special election to name a new president as soon as possible." She smiled at the camera without humor, turned, and left the room.

Sei muted the TV and translated what the prime minister had said. When he finished, Treavor spoke.

"So, she didn't say anything about a shoot-out at the cemetery?"

Sei shook his head. "Not a word, and nothing about how Teodorin died."

"I'll be damned," said Jake.

Then Treavor's cell chimed. It was Janick.

"Hey, Ted."

"Hey, Ted, yourself. What the hell happened? We've been calling both of you since yesterday."

"Sorry, we didn't get any calls, and I'm not sure why. But we have been pretty busy. Did you see Prime Minister Manuela Botey on TV?"

"No, we're in Rwanda."

"Well, both Nguema and his son have been eliminated, so Botey is taking control of the government for now."

There was a long pause. "Our friends here say that's a good thing."

"Yes, that's what's being said here too. But we still need to get out of here, and Jake has a fractured wrist. Can you help?"

"Sure thing. I'll get to work on getting you two extracted."

"Good. Let us know as soon as possible."

Ted put his government connections to work posthaste. At the end of the day, Michelle Obama called Manuela Botey, who was very willing to let young Jake, the financial planner, out of the country.

A day later, Sei and Miguel said their goodbyes and Jake and Treavor boarded the HS jet. Jake had learned it was good to have friends in high places, as Botey's personal physician had been dispatched to set his wrist.

It was a new day in Equatorial Guinea. By decree of the prime minister, all political prisoners were set free. Sales of gin and beer that day set new records. Nine months later, the small African nation had a mini baby boom. Not a single male baby was named Teodorin.

4

THE HS GANG LANDED in Washington, D.C. Ted and Chip were brought up to speed on the events at the cemetery on the long flight over. Everyone involved was happy, except Jake, whose wrist was still hurting.

Treavor arrived at his home in South Minneapolis, unpacked, did some laundry, cracked open a Coke, and checked his landline voice mail. There were a few calls—two solicitations, one for driveway sealing services, one for tree-trimming services, and one from someone named Thomas Bates from the University of Minnesota, following up on his leave of absence. *Hmm ... not someone I have dealt with before.* He called the number.

"Hello," Dickie Beasley said.

"Um ... this is Dr. Treavor Storm. You left a message. Something about my leave of absence?"

"Yes. Are you back in the States, Dr. Storm?"

"Um ... yes, I'm at home now, but what is this about?"

"Actually, we wondered whether you were coming back to the university," Dickie lied.

Treavor hesitated. "Who are you again?"

Dickie hung up.

Treavor looked at his phone, then redialed the number. No answer. He pursed his lips and called the university's general phone number. "Excuse me, but do you have a listing for a Thomas Bates?"

A pause. "No, sir. There's no one at the university by that name. There's a Silva Bates in the English Department and Dr. Ned Bates in the History Department, but no Thomas. Sorry, sir."

"That's OK, ma'am. Have a nice day," said Treavor, then he sat for a moment. *Huh. What was that all about? Strange. Oh, well.*

Treavor's looked around and grinned happily. *It's good to be home. A dawn run in the morning will get rid of the jet lag. But right now, it's time for food and a Coca-Cola or two. When Travis gets here, we can go for a grocery run.*

❖❖❖❖❖

Dickie Beasley smiled a killer's smile as he tossed his burner phone out the window of his van. *So, Dr. Storm is back home. Outstanding.* Now for the next stage of his operation, which was abducting his younger brother, Travis. Dickie had scouted out Treavor's home and had watched Travis leave for work more than a week ago. He followed him to St. David's Center in Minnetonka. That evening, he returned at 4 p.m. to see when Travis left, which was just after 5.

Dickie grunted as he thought about his recent purchase of a stun gun, courtesy of Amazon--a Taser professional series—the best they offered—at $1,499. Not cheap, but well worth it, given the rewards if this deal worked out.

He headed to the Original Pancake House for a late lunch of corned beef hash and three eggs looking at you, with blueberry pancakes on the side. At 3:45, he left for St. David's Center, pulled into the parking lot, and spotted Travis' car. There was an open spot next to it.. He parked his van there, got into the back, opened the sliding side doors, took his stun gun out, and waited.

Late that afternoon, Travis received a call from Treavor. He was back in town and wanted Travis to hit the McDonald's drive-through and get a couple of Big Macs, super-size fries, and a strawberry shake, then maybe go to the grocery store for him.

After work, he waved to the receptionist and headed out to the parking lot, car keys in hand. He frowned at the white van that was parked overly close to him. *Jeez, there are plenty of other parking spots, so why did some jerk need to squeeze me in? Oh, well.*

He turned sideways, put his hands on his car, and sidestepped toward the driver's door. As he passed the van's doors, he realized they were open. He sensed movement in the van, then he jerked, stunned, falling forward onto his car.

Dickie leaned forward, grabbed Travis by his hair, and yanked him into the van. He quickly closed the doors with a thud, hopped into the driver's seat, and headed out. He proceeded left onto Minnetonka Boulevard, past the police and fire station, then up to Interstate 494 North. Next, he turned off and drove to his home on the outskirts of Coon

Rapids. He pulled into the garage and exhaled, adrenaline coursing through his veins.

Travis hadn't moved, so Dickie tossed him over his shoulder and moved into his kitchen. He flopped Travis down in a chair, then wrapped his legs, torso, and arms with duct tape. Next, he gagged him with a mouth ball gag--a red, perforated ball the size of a golf ball with a black strap that went around the back of his head. It was only $9.99 on Amazon. *Boy, you can get anything on Amazon.*

He put a black sleep mask over Travis' eyes, stepped back, and surveyed his handiwork with satisfaction.

He had been saving his last jolt of meth just for this occasion. He fired up a pipe and enjoyed the familiar euphoria. He inhaled again and felt his self-confidence growing by leaps and bounds. Dickie needed to hit something, and by God, Travis was handy. So he reached over and backhanded him on the side of his face, then once more, then again. *That felt good. Too soon to kill the kid, though--I need him for a few days.*

Dickie headed into his living room and fired up a first-person shooter game on his Xbox. *Yeah, death, destruction, and mayhem. Too bad it isn't real. You know, those dudes who walked into their high schools had the right idea. Shoot the motherfuckers. Bo Turner, the goddamned captain of the football team, would go first. Fucking asshole. Oh, and Brittany Olsen, his girlfriend. So fucking stuck up, thought she was God's gift to the human race. Long, blond hair, beautiful, and wouldn't give me the time of day. I'd rape her first, then kill her. Yep.* Then the game started, and he amused himself with killing everything in front of him.

❖❖❖❖❖

Travis woke up, having no idea where he was. He couldn't see a thing. There was a terrible odor in the air, a mixture of rotten eggs and cat urine. He tried to move, but he was apparently bound to a chair. *What in the world is this all about? One moment, I'm in the parking lot at St. David's Center, and now I'm here ... wherever the hell here is. Son of a bitch!*

It was after dawn when Dickie woke up. He still had the game controller in his hand, the TV frozen in front of him. He was slumped on his beat-up couch and didn't feel good. His body ached as if he had been beaten. He felt like tossing his cookies while simultaneously having a craving for ... something. He pushed himself upright, and his head swayed. He was totally exhausted, but he had been there before. He sucked in a deep breath and winced. *Meth hangover. Getting worse each time.*

Dickie stood up and tottered into the kitchen, hungry. He stopped in the doorway with a start. There was a guy in a chair, taped and bound with duct tape, a red gag in his mouth, and a black sleeping mask covering his eyes. *What the fuck? Oh, yeah. I kidnapped this dude yesterday. But who the fuck is he? Hmm ... I need to think, but damn, I'm hungry.*

Dickie went to the refrigerator, opened it, and winced. There was an open container of something that was sprouting green and pinkish mold. He saw a few bottles of Budweiser, some shriveled apples, and some condiments in the door, including a jar of Famous Dave's Pickle Spears. He opened the pickle jar and began to eat while staring at the man seated across from him. He was finishing his third pickle when it dawned on him. *Travis Storm, brother of Dr. Treavor Storm, the invisible dude. I snatched him from a parking lot, and he is going to make me rich.*

Dickie was finishing the jar of pickles when he knocked it over, the juice running out toward Travis' lap. He stood up and headed to the bedroom, fell onto the bed, and was out before his head hit the pillow.

Travis had fallen asleep just before dawn, and slept through Dickie's kitchen visit, which was just as well. When he awakened, his face hurt where he had been struck, but he had no recollection of being hit. The rotten egg odor still lingered, but he thought he smelled something like pickles, and his crotch was wet as well. *Did I wet himself while I slept? Did I pee pickle juice? What the fuck was happening? This is nuts. Absolutely fucking crazy nuts!*

❖❖❖❖❖

Travis hadn't come home from St. David's the night before, and Treavor was frantic. He had called his sister, the cop, but got her machine.

Then he called his parents, and his mother answered. "No, I haven't seen him. But he has a new girlfriend, so maybe he is with her. I don't know her number, but her name's Amber."

He tried his brother Thomas next.

"Nope, I haven't heard from Travis. How long has he been gone?"

"Since yesterday, Jake replied."

'This is very concerning. It isn't like Travis at all to just drop off the radar "Did you call Tanya?"

"Yes, no answer."

"Shit."

"Indeed."

"I'll see what I can find. Keep me posted."

"Sure, right."

Treavor got very little sleep that night, just like Travis. The next morning, all hell broke loose.

❖❖❖❖❖

Dickie woke up just after dawn, fully dressed, shoes and all. He was still achy, but not nearly as exhausted, and starving. He headed to the bathroom and did his business, then moved slowly to the kitchen, taking a new burner phone with him. Once in the kitchen, he paused. Travis was awake and moaning. Dickie grinned. "Well, well, Mr. Travis Storm, welcome to my humble abode."

Travis tried to reply, but the ball gag prevented it.

Dickie slithered to the refrigerator, but there was nothing that looked edible in it. He opened the freezer and pulled out a Red Baron pizza, deluxe. *Excellent. Breakfast.* He turned on the oven to 400 degrees, opened the pizza box, and threw it in the oven. *The hell with preheating. I'm hungry, dammit.*

He turned and looked at Travis. "I bet you're wondering what the fuck is going on. Just getting off work and headed home, and *poof!* You end up here." Dickie laughed wickedly. "You see, you have the honor of having a brother who is invisible, which is pretty goddamned cool, if you ask me. So, I watched you on the news with that babe from Channel 9, Samantha Henderson. Now, there's a babe I'd like to fuck six ways to Sunday. I bet she'd love it. Who knows, maybe when I'm rich she'll go out with me. We could get married and have all sorts of kids."

Travis grunted. *Damn, this guy is demented. I just hope he's not a murderer.*

Dickie cocked his head. "But first things first, sonny boy. I'm going to call your brother and tell him what I want him to do. You just sit there, and you won't get hurt if he cooperates. *Capiche?*"

Travis shook his head vehemently as Dickie dialed Treavor's number.

Treavor was still in bed, awake, when his cell chimed. He didn't recognize the number, but he picked it up anyway. "Hello, this is Dr. Treavor Storm."

"How's your day going so far, doc?" Dickie asked.

"Huh?"

"Well, I hate to tell you, but it ain't gonna get better unless you do exactly as I tell you. You see, my friend, I have your brother Travis sitting across from me, and I'd like you to do a small favor for me. If you do, he won't get hurt—or worse."

Treavor drew in a breath as sharp as a rifle crack. "What are you talking about?"

"Goddammit, doc. Aren't you paying attention? I have Travis, your baby brother. You do what I tell you, or I'll fucking kill him," Dickie said angrily.

"Okay, I'm listening. What do you want me to do?"

"All right, that's better. I need you to use your special gift to make a visit to one of my favorite stores in Wayzata. I bet you've been there—Gunderson's Jewelers, used to be J.B. Hudson. Nice shop, great assortment of diamonds and watches. They actually have a 201 carat Chopard watch worth 25 mil. So, here's the deal. You steal a bunch of diamonds, along with the watch, and he goes free. Fuckin' easy-peasy. Oh, by the way, no cops or your brother dies."

Treavor sighed. "How do I know this isn't bullshit?"

"Oh, doc, ye of little faith. Hold on," he said.

Dickie removed the gag from Travis' mouth, as well as the mask that covered his eyes. He had decided to kill Travis when this was over, so he didn't give a shit if Travis saw him. "Hey, buddy, say hi to your brother."

"Treavor, get me the fuck out of here!" Travis blurted at the top of his lungs.

Treavor trembled with anger, his blood boiling. "Are you OK, Travis?"

"No, I'm not. Do what he says, or he's going to kill me!"

Dickie yanked the phone away from Travis. "Now that young man is smart. Listen to what he says. Call me when you have the watch and a bag of jewels. I need at least 100 million dollars in gems. Use your imagination, doc. It'll be fun. Hell, take a few gems for your troubles. I'm a generous guy." Then he laughed hysterically. "Call me when it's done, let's say a day from now. I'll entertain your brother in the meantime. Make me proud, doc."

❖❖❖❖❖

Treavor lay in bed totally stunned, pinching himself to ensure he wasn't dreaming. He swung his legs over the side of the bed and sat there for a moment or two, staring out the window. *Another kidnapping—first Jake's Beth Ann and now Travis. Shit, shit, shit. The kidnapper said no cops. But that's what they always say, right? To hell with him. I need Tanya to be part of this.* He dialed her cell, but there was no answer.

He stood up, headed to the bathroom, and quickly did his morning ritual. When he was done, he decided to call Easton Carter at the FBI, then stopped. *Hold on. Why not call Jake Silver in case someone needs to be killed? He'd certainly be the man for the job.*

Jake answered on the first ring. He was with his friend Omar Carter, hashing out a plan to rescue Beth Ann. Jake listened patiently as Treavor brought him up to speed on the kidnapping of Travis. "Holy shit, I can't believe this! Is there like a 'buy one, get one free' for kidnappers?" He didn't laugh. "Treavor, are you at home now?"

"Yes."

"We will be there in forty minutes."

They were there in thirty. Jake introduced Omar, a bear of a man, former member of the Green Bay Packers and a future hall-of-famer. As for Dr. Storm's invisibility, Omar took it in stride. "Hell, Jake can point and say "Just die," and people do it," he said. "You being invisible isn't any stranger than that."

"So, this ass-wipe didn't give you any clue who he was?" inquired Jake.

"Not at all, but man, he sounded kind of out there, like he was coming down from something. Spacey," Treavor said.

Omar shook his head. "Well, great. A druggie who's off his rocker and willing to kill. Luckily, we have just the man here to take care of the shithead."

Jake nodded slightly.

"Should I actually steal this stuff or just set up a meet as if I did?" Treavor asked.

"Do as he says," Jake replied. "You don't want to make him suspicious. But whatever happens, we'll get this guy and make him pay." He smiled wryly. "Besides, I've never seen a 25-million-dollar watch. I'd like to try it on."

Finally, everyone laughed.

❖❖❖❖❖

That night, the three of them headed to the Gunderson's Jewelers store. They parked on the Wayzata Promenade Center's ramp and entered the store. They were greeted by a handsome woman dressed in a pale blue blazer that matched her eyes. She scanned Jake and Omar, sizing them up in an instant. *Moderately rich. Less than $10 million.* She gave them her second-best smile. "Welcome, gentlemen. How may I be of service to you?"

Jake stepped toward her. "I understand you have a Chopard 201-carat watch."

She gave a little start, revising her initial assessment. "Yes, sir, absolutely. Please, allow me to show you."

She moved to the end of the long counter where a dazzling array of watches were displayed, including every type of Rolex. In the center of the glass case, on a four-inch pedestal, sat the Chopard in all its glory. It was a sight to behold, with a diamond-studded wristband. On the watch itself were huge diamonds—white, brilliant, and yellow, and even an orangish-pink one. The woman reached into the cabinet and very carefully extracted the timepiece. She set it down as if it were the crown jewels.

Jake nodded. "Very impressive. I was thinking of getting it for my fiancée as a wedding present. Do you think it's appropriate for such an occasion?"

The woman sucked in a greedy breath. "Oh my, yes, absolutely. We can, of course, adjust it to her wrist size."

Jake leaned forward and whispered, "She's the daughter of a Saudi Prince. I'd actually be buying it with his money."

The woman's eyes popped open and she flashed a Cheshire cat grin. "Oh my, such a generous father!"

"Oh yes, he is. Unless you piss him off, in which case you'd disappear." He pointed at the watch. "May I try it on?"

"Oh yes, sir, absolutely." She removed the watch from its case and presented it to Jake like it was the last watch on earth.

Jake slipped it on. The jeweled watch sparkled under the bright lights of the shop. He held it out for Omar to see. "Well, buddy, what do you think?"

Omar laughed, his deep, bass voice filling the shop. "Maybe you should get two, one for each of you!"

Jake nodded in agreement. "By God, that's a great idea. I'll have to ask the prince. Hell, maybe he'd like one as well."

The clerk nearly fainted. Jake gave her his best smile. "Can you get three of them?"

The woman trembled with excitement. "Yes, sir! Absolutely," she replied with glee.

Jake removed the watch and handed it back to her. "Excellent. Let me ask the prince, and I'll get back to you."

She held the precious watch in her hand. "Um ... sir, can I get your name, please?" she asked.

Jake pursed his lips. "Yes, Amos Andy."

The woman nodded, her eyes wide open. "Can you give me a phone number?"

Jake shook his head. "I'll call you if you don't mind. I don't give out my number."

The woman nodded immediately. "Yes, sir, I understand. Please give me a few days to acquire the watches."

"Great! Thanks for the showing." Jake turned to leave, winking at Omar, who was smothering a laugh.

The woman stood as tall as she could. "YES, SIR! Have a wonderful evening!"

On the walk back to the car, Treavor said, "My God, Jake, you're a cruel dude. The woman had visions of retiring on the commission she would've made."

Omar chuckled. "A freakin' Saudi Prince? Are you kidding me?"

"Yeah, I know, but you have to admit the whole thing was fun," Jake replied.

5

DICKIE JUMPED UP. "Burning pizza! Crap-ola." He opened the oven door and smoke billowed out. He turned on the exhaust fan and slammed the stove door shut. Travis laughed, and Dickie started to smack him.

"Hey, stop it, goddammit!" Travis hollered. "Listen, I've got a few bucks in my wallet. Why don't you order a pizza?"

Dickie's eyes widened. "Cool." Then he slid around the back of Travis' chair and dug the wallet out of his back pocket. He opened it and frowned. *Shit, not enough for meth.* He spread the wallet open—driver's license, a picture of a nice-looking girl, a Blue Cross health care card, a COVID-19 vaccination card, and a yellow Detello's coupon good for $5 off a purchase of $30 or more, and that was it. No credit cards and no ATM card.

"Fuck me," Dickie cried out. "Don't you have a fucking ATM card?"

"Hell no. Too tempting. Listen, man, I really need to use the bathroom or I'm going to shit myself."

"So go ahead and shit yourself. What the fuck do I care?" Dickie barked.

"Aw, come on. Do you really want to eat pizza with my shit smelling up the room?"

"All right, have it your way.." He took out a paring knife and cut Travis loose. Travis got up, stretched, and tottered on cramped legs to the bathroom, which was adjacent to the kitchen. He began to close the door, and Dickie's voice rang out. "Leave the fucking door open, asshole."

Travis grumbled but complied. The bathroom was a half bath ... no shower or tub--and smelled of shit and urine. The pedestal sink was covered with grime, and the retro floor--with eight-inch black-and-white tiles, many cracked and chipped--was worse than the sink. It looked like it hadn't been cleaned in years. The grout had been white or gray, but was now mostly a yellowish green. The toilet wasn't any better, and Travis decided not to sit, squatting instead over the fetid bowl. He flushed twice, turned, and left quickly before he lost his appetite completely.

❖❖❖❖❖

Beth Ann Noble had left her apartment on her wedding day. Just when she was about to get into her car, two short, muscular, Korean men appeared and lifted her up as if she were a feather, carrying her away and into a Lincoln limousine, wedding dress and all. She was so stunned she didn't even scream. That came later. She was given an injection, and the next day was lost to her. What followed was a long plane ride, another injection, and no wedding.

Now she was sitting on the beach at Kim Jong-un's resort, Wonsan, a massive seaside resort that could hold up to six of Donald Trump's Mar-a-Lago resorts. It housed multiple swimming pools, tennis courts, soccer fields, water slides, a sports stadium, and groomed beaches. On the Sea of Japan bobbed yachts, dinner boats, and lots of sailboats. It was a wonderful spot to spend a vacation ... unless you were being held captive. Then, not so much. Two guards stood ten feet away from Beth Ann, and two more stood at attention behind her. They were all dressed in Mao suits, with long dark pants and black leather shoes, despite the scorching-hot sun.

She was making do by having her fourth mai tai. *When in doubt, get sauced, right? Hell, I'm all cried out by now. I screamed until the proverbial cows came home, for all the good it did.*

On the other hand, she was being treated like a princess now that she was here. She could have anything she wanted to eat, drink, smoke, or snort. She had learned that this whole thing was about something that Kim Jong-un needed Jake to do, and she had a pretty good idea what that involved Jake's killing power. Once he did what was asked of him, she'd be released, flown back to the States, and gifted ten million dollars. Or so they said. She thought that was bullshit, so she sipped her cocktail, wiped away a stray tear with the back of her hand, and pined for Jake, her lover and soulmate.

◆◆◆◆◆

Jake, Treavor, and Omar were sitting in the CōV restaurant beside Lake Minnetonka, with a railroad track running between the building and the shoreline. They were on the patio, twenty yards from the track.

Jake was gazing out at the lake, thinking about Beth Ann. He missed her terribly. She was his support system, and she stood by him when he was exercising his new power--not questioning him at all. He knew he needed to make something happen, but he couldn't just keep on killing people for Kim Jong-un.

Omar glanced at Jake. "What'cha thinking about, Jake?"

"Aw, just about Beth Ann, wondering whether she's even still alive."

Omar shook his head. "Don't even go there. Why wouldn't she be? You have been doing everything that asshole Kim Jong-un has required."

"Yeah, so far, but this can't go on forever. What if he wants me to kill the president next?"

The men sat silent for a minute, then Treavor changed the subject. "So, guys, I'm thinking tomorrow, about an hour or so before closing time, I go into the jewelry store and see what the routine is. They must have a safe where the watches and high-ticket items are stored overnight. If so, I'll try to get the combination and open it once everyone goes home. I'll get the rest of the most expensive pieces, then I'm not sure whether I should leave or stay all night. There must be some sort of alarm, don't you think?"

Jake stroked his chin. "Boy, I have no idea. How about if you play it by ear? We can hang around for a few hours, and if you decide to leave, we'll pick you up. If you decide to stay, we'll be there just before the store opens."

Treavor nodded. "Okay. We can play it by ear."

❖❖❖❖❖

Treavor scooted into the store a half hour before closing. The woman who had tended to Jake the day before wasn't working. Instead, a tall woman with bedroom eyes and the longest eyelashes Treavor had ever seen was on duty. There was also a stocky clerk in a black tuxedo showing wedding rings to a thirty-something couple.

Treavor detoured around them, noticing that the Chopard was still in its display case. He paused at a showcase of necklaces, including one with twenty or more diamonds as big as his thumbnail strung together on a thick gold chain. Treavor guessed that the store held over $50 million in gems.

He continued down a narrow hall. On the left were the restrooms, and farther back was an office. Inside, an obese man was standing in front of a mahogany desk that looked like it was worth more than Treavor's home. The fellow was clad in a navy-blue suit that must have been tailored when he was twenty pounds lighter, and a garish flower-print tie. As he chatted on an old-fashioned phone, his smile revealed a mouthful of yellowed teeth. "Yes, ma'am, absolutely. We will put it aside for you immediately."

Treavor flashed a pleased grin as he saw a large safe in the far corner with an old-fashioned rotary lock. *That'll make this easy. All I have to do is remember the combination when this guy opens the safe.*

Ten minutes later, Treavor was standing in a corner, watching the tall woman lock the glass door of the shop. Tuxedo Man locked all the cases, except for the diamond necklace case and watch display. He reached in and extracted the velvet-lined trays and stacked them, placing the Chopard in its case on top of the stack.

Treavor quickly moved ahead of him to the office and was standing in the corner when the clerk set everything on the boss's desk and tipped an imaginary hat at him.

"Have a nice evening," the boss said without enthusiasm.

"You too, sir," the clerk replied, and walked out, closing the door behind him.

The boss moved to the safe, squatted down, and turned the dial. Treavor was right behind him and watched, memorizing the numbers—3 right, 8 left, 9 right, 1 left. The boss opened the safe and placed the stack on the top shelf, closed it, spun the dial, then went to a closet to retrieve a tan topcoat. He slipped it on, whirled around, and vacated his office, leaving the door open.

Treavor waited a few minutes, then moved back toward the store entrance. Everyone was gone.

He strode back to the office and up to the safe. Treavor's heart was in his mouth, an adrenaline surge making his hands shake. He inhaled and blew it out slowly, trying to calm himself. "Relax, just relax," he said to himself. He bent over and spun the dial—3 right, 8 left, 9 right, 1 left. When he heard a click, he pulled the handle and the door was open.

Treavor trembled with excitement, then paused. *Damn, I forgot to bring anything to put these things in! Man, how stupid was that?*

He turned and saw a walnut wastebasket next to the desk. Treavor dumped it on the boss's chair and carefully put his haul into it. He picked it up, and it disappeared.

Treavor left the office and moved to the front door. There was a deadbolt with a knob. No need for a key. When he turned the knob and opened the door, a loud siren shrieked. He quickly closed the door behind him and hurried away.

He bolted into the parking lot and down the street toward the restaurant. He spotted Jake's car in the parking lot, opened the back door, and slid in.

"Whew!" he exclaimed to his startled partners as he placed the wastebasket on the seat next to him. Omar reached over from the passenger seat and flashed a ten-megawatt smile. "Holy smokes, you did it!" he exclaimed.

"I did, so let's get the heck out of here."

As they cruised away, Omar said, "I hate to admit it, but grand theft is a kind of rush!"

❖❖❖❖❖

After the pizza was delivered and devoured, the rest of the night was spent with Travis bound and gagged on Dickie's threadbare sofa. The next day, there was enough money left over for Dickie to order Taco Bell delivery, so they dined on Dorito Taco Supremes while watching *The Good, the Bad, and the Ugly.* Travis thought that his captor had two of those categories covered before he fell asleep in the middle of the flick. He hadn't slept much in the past day.

That evening, Dickie's cell buzzed. It was Treavor, saying he had the loot.

"Hallelujah!" Dickie roared.

"So now what?" asked Treavor.

"There's an abandoned Shell station at the edge of Stacy. We will be behind it at midnight tonight. You meet us there. I'll have a gun to this boy's head, and I swear I'll kill him. You set the loot on the dirt, back off fifty feet, and get on the ground. I know I can't see you, so just keep talking. Once I have the stuff, I'll let him go. If there are cops around, I'll shoot Travis, then myself."

"You don't care about dying?"

"Sure I do, but you're more worried about your brother here. I'll gamble with my life because you aren't going to let him die. Am I right?"

"Of course. I did what you told me, so let's just get this over with."

"Now you're talking. See you at midnight. Just you, no one else, or else..."

"Yeah, I know, kill my brother."

Dickie snickered and hung up.

Travis had been listening. "Would you really kill me?"

"Fuck yes. You see, I'm so fucking hooked on meth that I'll be dead within five years. This way, it'll be the best five years of my life. Getting high every day, beaches, and tons of women, then a hell of a funeral when I croak. Prop me in a chair with my pipe, and have a fucking party, maybe even a rock band. Do you think Bon Jovi would play?" Then Dickie laughed crazily.

Travis' heart pounded, and he was barely able to breathe. *This man is certifiably nuts.*

❖❖❖❖❖

After Treavor's call with Dickie ended, he looked at Jake and Omar. "Holy cow, this guy is something else!"

Omar nodded. "Oh yes, I've seen meth addicts in and out of the hospital I used to work at. They live for the high."

Jake pursed his lips. "Well, if he wants to die, maybe I can accommodate him."

"Jake, don't you ever just get tired of killing people?" Treavor asked.

"Hey, he said he could kill Travis, didn't he?"

"Well, he said he'd rather not."

Jake scowled. "OK, fine, my naive friend, have it your way. Omar and I will get some sleep. You can just let us know how it ends up."

"Aw, come on, Jake. I need you to be there. It's just that I hate all this killing."

Jake shrugged. "Hey, pal, it's what I do. No one is asking you to kill anyone."

Treavor sighed heavily. "Yeah, you're right."

"You bet I am. Now let's go check this place out. I want to be in place well before this fucker gets there. We'll take my car. Okay?"

"Sure, that sounds good."

"Count me in," said Omar.

They headed up Interstate Highway 35 North and pulled off at the Stacy exit, then proceeded to the far side of town to the deserted Shell station with its familiar yellow-and-red sign. There were numerous bullet holes in the sign, courtesy of frustrated deer hunters, that loomed over the spots where the pumps had stood.

Jake drove around to the back of the station and parked fifty feet from where a white van sat waiting. Jake looked at Treavor, who was holding the sack of loot and asked, "Are you ready for this?"

Treavor groaned. "Do I have a choice?"

❖❖❖❖❖

At 11:30 p.m., Dickie had Travis in the back of his van, wrists and ankles bound in duct tape. He took a Donald Trump Halloween mask and put it on the seat next to him, and off they went. An hour later, they arrived at the Shell station, drove around the back, and waited. It wasn't long before another car pulled in.

Treavor opened the passenger door, got out, and walked toward Dickie's van. Dickie was standing next to it, wearing the Trump mask and holding a gun to the back of Travis' head. "Who the hell is driving? I said for you to come alone," he growled.

"Hey, what makes you think I can drive? I'm freakin' invisible. I'd get pulled over in a heartbeat," Treavor replied.

Dickie squinted and pursed his lips. "Oh, I guess that makes sense. So, where's the loot?"

"Here in my hand."

Treavor set the bag on the ground. It appeared as if from nowhere, and Dickie whooped. "Pick it up and bring it forward another forty feet."

Treavor bent down, and the bag disappeared, which unnerved Dickie. Then it reappeared.

Dickie grunted with pleasure. "OK, back up to the car and keep talking. If you have a gun, I'll shoot your baby brother."

Treavor did as he was told. He called out, "Travis, are you okay? Did he hurt you?"

Dickie pulled Travis backward. He squatted down and picked the bag up, then stood up again. With the gun now back in place up against Travis' head, he began to back up to where he thought he'd be out of the range of a handgun. Then he laughed wickedly.

Jake leaned out of the window and shouted, "Travis, drop down—now!"

Travis did so without hesitation.

Then Jake pointed at Dickie's head and shrieked "Just die!"

Dickie collapsed on top of Travis like a sack of potatoes. Both men were still, and Jake stood breathless. *My God, did I kill Travis?*

Then Dickie moved, and Jake shook his head. *Is he still alive? Have I lost the power?* But it was just Travis moving Dickie off him, and Jake sighed with relief.

Travis glanced down at Dickie's corpse, Trump mask still in place, then turned to look at Jake, who was striding toward him. "How the hell did you do that?" he asked, trembling.

Treavor smiled. "Travis, meet my new partner, Jake Silver. He has a very unique talent."

"Like saying 'Just die' and people do?"

Jake nodded. "That's it exactly." Then he laughed and held his hand out. "Despite the circumstances, it's nice to finally meet you, Travis."

Travis sucked in a breath. "Same here —and thank you."

6

BEFORE LEAVING THE gas station, they propped Dickie up in the driver's seat of his van. Travis grabbed the Trump mask for a macabre souvenir.

At Treavor's home, Travis changed into a clean set of clothes. He also used the facilities and felt much better. The gang was sitting in Treavor's kitchen, drinking a beverage of their choice, listening to Travis talk about how he was snatched out of the parking lot of St. David's Center.

"There was a white van next to me at St. David's when I got off work, and I didn't give it a second thought. The side doors were open, and when I went by them, I got zapped. Never saw it coming. Next thing I knew, I was bound and gagged and at this dude's house." He touched his injured head. "He duct-taped me to a kitchen chair, then put a blindfold on me and a fancy gag. After a while, he went in the next room and was smoking something that smelled like rotten eggs. Then he just came back and whacked me for no fucking reason. The dude was a certifiable wacko. Man, I thought I was a goner."

Jake leaned forward. "Yeah, me too. I thought I might have killed you along with the guy."

"Lucky for me you've got good aim, right?" Travis eyed the sack. "Hey, what's in there?"

Treavor grunted. "Aw, not much ... maybe 150 million dollars in diamonds and a really nice watch."

"Hey, man, can I see? I need a new watch."

Jake laughed, then carefully removed the contents from the sack. He opened the case that held the watch and slid it across the table. "Here you go."

"Holy shit!" Travis exclaimed. He picked the watch up, amazed at how much it sparkled under the kitchen lights. He put it on and gazed in admiration at the ornate timepiece. "This is incredible. Can I have it?"

The rest of the group laughed, and Jake said, "Only if you have twenty-five million dollars."

Travis gulped and removed the watch. He reached over and held up a diamond necklace. "Boy, this is something else. Maybe my new girlfriend would like it."

Treavor grunted. "A new girlfriend?"

Travis' face turned pink. "Yeah, she works at St. David's and is a former student, just like me."

"Nice. What's her name?"

"Amber Nelson."

"Well, good for you, Travis. I'd like to meet her."

"Yeah, she's anxious to meet my invisible brother." He paused. "So, can I give this to her?"

"Yeah, right." The necklace disappeared from Travis' hand as Treavor snatched it away.

"Hey, bro, I darn near got killed. Don't I get anything?"

Treavor thought for a moment. "How about if I give you my Camry?"

Travis' eyes opened wide. "Really?"

"Sure, why not. Heck, if you have a girlfriend, you're going to need wheels!"

"Woo-hoo! That's super-duper. Thanks, Treavor!"

"You're welcome."

Omar contemplated the loot still on the table. "What do we do about this?"

"Return it, of course," Treavor replied.

"Darn, that's no fun," Travis said.

❖❖❖❖❖

The next day, Jake drove Treavor back to Wayzata and the jewelry store, but not before he stopped at a Quick Trip for a tuna sandwich and a small carton of chocolate milk.

Treavor picked up the sack of loot and the treats and headed into the store. It was busy, and he ambled down the hall and back to the office. The boss was on the phone again, apparently with his insurance company.

"Are you kidding me? That's not even half of what I lost! You get your assessor over here today. I'll have all the receipts and the police report ready. There's no way I'm going bankrupt because you won't pay up. I'll sue you first."

The boss was facing away from Treavor, so he put the sack on the desk along with the tuna sandwich and chocolate milk, then stepped back into the corner.

The boss yelled, "Bullshit!" and disconnected the phone, then turned and froze. "What the hell?" He plopped down in his chair, then put his hand up and scratched his bald head. He reached out and gingerly pulled the sack toward him, as if it held a bomb or a batch of snakes. He carefully opened it and yelped. He extracted the Chopard case and extracted the watch. Then he slowly emptied out the rest of the sack's contents and lined them up on his desk.

He sat with his hands on his massive belly, twiddling his thumbs with an astonished expression on his face. Then he eyed the tuna sandwich. He brought it up to his nose and sniffed it. He nodded approvingly and took a massive bite, smiling happily as he chewed.

Treavor smiled as well and left. *Mission accomplished.*

❖❖❖❖❖

Two days later, Treavor was finishing up his dawn run. He walked across his lawn, kicking up dew sparkles. It was shaping up to be a wonderful day. The sun was peeking its head up in the east, and the pale-blue morning sky was peppered with brilliant white clouds. *Good day to be alive.*

Afterward, he headed down to the basement to do some bench presses and free-weights. After showering and eating breakfast, he was about to read the Bible when his cell buzzed. It was Jake.

"Hey, Jake."

"Hi, Treavor. How are you doing?"

"I'm great. Had a nice run this morning and pumped a little iron."

"Good for you. Listen, I got an email from Kim Jong-un for one last assignment."

"Aw, darn. Well, you knew that was a possibility."

"Yeah, I know, but I didn't expect this."

"Expect what?"

"He wants me to assassinate the prime minister of Israel."

"Oh my God!"

"Yeah, you can say that again."

"What are you going to do?"

"Well, I'm certainly not going to kill him. But Omar has an idea, and we would like to come over and talk about it."

"Sure, absolutely. When?"

"How about now?"

"Uh ... sure, OK."

"OK, great. We'll be there in forty minutes."

"All right."

Holy cow! The prime minister of Israel? That's crazy.

Twenty minutes later, Omar pulled into Treavor's driveway driving Jake's classic red Jaguar XKE. He and Jake climbed out, headed up to the house, and rang the doorbell.

Treavor opened the door and peeked out at them, then at the Jag. "Holy smollies!" he exclaimed. "I have one just like that, but mine is yellow."

Omar turned and eyed the car. "I wish it were mine, but it belongs to Jake."

The men headed to the kitchen. "Got any Diet Coke in your fridge, Treavor?" Jake asked.

"You bet."

Jake and Omar stood in Treavor's kitchen drinking Diet Cokes while Treavor drank his usual regular Coke. "Okay, what do you want to do, Jake?" Treavor asked.

"What I'm thinking is that we recruit Dennis Norman and some of his buddies to head back to North Korea and play a basketball game or two for Kim Jong-un. Then we go with him and rescue Beth Ann."

Treavor sniffed. "That's it?"

"Well, yeah. With your help, we can do it," Jake said. "I'm pretty sure Homeland Security can reach out to Dennis and recruit him and his former NBA buddies. The last time they played, it was at Kim's beach resort in Wonsan. Kim is there most of the time now, and I have a hunch it's where he's keeping Beth Ann."

Omar grinned. "Better yet, how about if the president reaches out to him? You know they're buddies. Heck, Dennis tried to date his daughter before she got married."

Jake raised an eyebrow. "I had no idea. I don't see how Dennis could refuse. But we need this done quickly, or I'll need to assassinate the prime minister of Israel."

Treavor said "Wait...what?"

"Just kidding," Jake replied with a thin smile.

Jake picked up his cell and called Ted Janick, who answered immediately.

"Hello, Jake, how are you doing?"

"I've been better, Ted. I just got an assignment from our friend in North Korea. Guess who he wants me to kill now?"

"I don't know ... our president and the entire Congress?"

"Nope, the prime minister of Israel."

"Yeah, that makes sense, come to think of it. Dammit."

"Well, I'm certainly not going to do that, but Omar has a great idea. We could set up a basketball game in North Korea, and we would tag along with the team. We then would split off and try to find Beth Ann and rescue her."

"Hmm ... you know what? That's a decent idea. Heck, it's worth a try, right? But it would need to be done quickly."

"Yeah, we agree."

"OK, I'll call Da Boss right away and see what he thinks. If he likes the idea, he might reach out to the president. Stay tuned, okay?"

"Sure, will do. Thanks."

"Don't thank me yet."

Four hours later, Ted called back. "The president says he'll reach out to Norman, and he'll do it—or else."

"That's great! Thank the president for me," Jake replied.

"You can thank him yourself. He wants you all at the White House the day after tomorrow to go over the plan."

"Well, that's great ... I think."

"Yeah. He also mentioned an assignment for you and Dr. Storm after you rescue Beth Ann. He's intrigued by the possibilities of the two of you teaming up."

"OK, as long as we don't get killed in North Korea," Jake said solemnly.

7

JAKE, TREAVOR, AND Omar were sitting in the waiting room outside the Oval Office. Tony Seiffer, the president's chief of staff, was sitting with them and chatting amicably with Treavor.

"So, you went out for a run last January, slipped on the ice in front of your home, and you've been invisible ever since?"

"Yup, that sums it up," Treavor replied.

"Extraordinary." Seiffer gestured at Jake. "And the two of you are now Homeland Security agents?"

"Yes, sir."

"This is amazing. Well, thank God you're both US citizens and not from some hostile nation!"

Then the door to the Oval Office opened, and the president stood in the doorway.

"Hey, guys, good to see you again. Come in. I want to introduce you to some friends of mine."

Jake chuckled quietly and looked at where Treavor was sitting. "Yeah, Treavor, good to see you," he whispered.

They all trooped into the famous office. The president walked around his desk. "Jake, Treavor, Mr. Carter, I'd like to introduce you to my friend Dennis Norman and his buddies Michael Forman and Charles Deckle. Also, our new friend, Giannis Antunopolous of the Milwaukee Bucks."

Jake and Treavor were stunned and froze in place, but Omar smiled and moved toward Giannis. "Hey, man, good to see you again," he said.

Giannis returned the smile, stood up--all 6-feet-11 of him--and stretched out his hand. "Hey, man, I heard you were coming. Good to see you too!"

The president cocked his head. "Oh, do you two know each other?"

Giannis nodded. "Omar invited a bunch of us to a suite at Lambeau Field for a Packers game."

Giannis moved toward Jake. "You must be Jake Silver. I understand your fiancée has been abducted by Dennis' buddy Kim Jong-un. Man, that sucks."

"Thank you. It was a shock, that's for sure," Jake replied.

"Well, we're all here to help in any way we can."

Norman pursed his lips and remained seated. "I suggested to the president that I could call him and ask him to release her. We're on really good terms, as you know. I bet he'd do it for me."

Seiffer spoke up. "Dennis, we thought about that, but what if he says no? Then he'd know something was up, and he might move the hostage—or worse."

Dennis shrugged. "Yeah, I guess. I just don't want to screw up my relationship with Kim."

The president leaned forward. "Well, dude, if you don't, you're going to screw up your relationship with me."

Dennis grimaced, but said nothing.

Then Michael Forman spoke up. "Hey, where is this invisible man? I still don't think I believe he's real."

"I'm right here," Treavor replied, and the world-famous basketball player jumped a few inches off his chair.

"Holy shit!" Forman exclaimed.

"Real enough for you?"

Forman nodded with wide-open eyes.

"By the way, nice to meet you all. I know Jake and Omar, and I really appreciate you doing this," Treavor said.

The president said, "Dennis, we need you to call Kim. Tell him that you have a group of ball players who are sympathetic to his cause and would like to come over and play. And tell him it needs to be soon, because NBA training camp is about to start."

The president glanced at his watch. "Listen, men, I need you to clear out of here. I have a meeting with a few senators. We're trying to push a bill through, and I need two more votes." Then he turned to Seiffer. "I need daily updates on this, and you're authorized to do whatever is necessary to make this happen."

The president turned and clasped Jake's hand. "I truly hope this works, Mr. Silver. You did a wonderful job supporting me in Russia with Kim's problem, and I'm indebted to you. Go with God, gentlemen."

"

8

BETH ANN WAS ONCE again sitting on the beach. She glanced at a group of beachgoers who were gathered around a dog that had a crab fastened to his nose. Everyone was standing around doing nothing at all. Beth Ann stood up, tossed her magazine down, and pushed through the onlookers. The dog, a medium-size puppy, was whimpering and shaking his head back and forth, attempting to dislodge the crab. Unfortunately, it was to no avail, and his snout was covered with blood.

Beth Ann crouched down next to the dog and gently stroked his back. "Easy now, puppy. Easy now." She reached up and massaged the back of his neck. "Come on, boy, let me help you." Beth Ann continued to rub the dog's neck, and the animal stopped shaking his head. He looked at Beth Ann, whimpering even louder. Beth Ann scratched the top of his head. "Stay still."

She grabbed the crab's claws with both hands and pried them off the dog, then tossed the crab into the surf. The puppy's whimpering subsided a bit, but he was obviously hurt, as the claws had dug a half inch into his nose.

She put her arms under the animal, picked him up, and stood up. Then she turned and headed for the main building. The onlookers parted to let her through, and a young Korean man stepped forward. He said something in Korean, then signaled for her to stop, pointing at the puppy, then at himself.

It was obviously his dog, so he slipped his hands under the dog and took him from her.

Next, he spun around and headed toward the building with Beth Ann shadowing him. Inside, the fellow turned to the left, hurried down a long hall, made a right turn at the end, and walked to the second door on the right. The sign on the side of the door had five characters underneath. He stopped, stepped aside, said something in Korean, and nodded toward the doorknob. Beth Ann nodded as well, so she opened the door and went in first, holding it open.

It was a clinic waiting room that was nearly empty. The man moved up to the counter where a receptionist frowned when she saw the dog. She shook her head and said something to the man. He shook his head as well and spoke loudly. It was evident that he wasn't happy. The woman replied, then raised her hands and shrugged, as if there was nothing she could do. The man responded vehemently with "*Eongteoli*," then Beth Ann laughed quietly. She knew a few Korean words, and that was one of them. It was translated roughly as "Bullshit."

The man sat down in a chair, stroking the dog's back affectionately. Beth Ann sat next to him. When the waiting room was completely empty the receptionist stood up and went through the door that opened into the back of the clinic.

A few moments later, she returned with a woman Beth Ann assumed was a nurse. The woman spoke to the man with the dog, and he nodded and followed her through the door. Beth Ann accompanied them.

In the examination room, the nurse peered at the dog, pursing her lips and murmuring with sympathy. Beth Ann heard the Korean word for "crab." The nurse turned, went to a cabinet, and came back with a sterile cloth and a bottle of saline. She spoke to the man, and he held the dog's head as she cleaned the wounds. She stood back and looked at Beth Ann, smiled tentatively, and said "Hello" in perfect English.

Beth Ann returned the smile. "Hello to you." Then she eyed the dog. "Excuse me, I'm a veterinarian. Would you consider giving the dog an antibiotic?"

The nurse held up a finger, then went out the door. Five minutes later, she came back with a syringe and a vial. She held it up for Beth Ann to view. Then she nodded at the man and asked him to hold his dog's hindquarters.

She squatted down and gave the pooch an injection, then stood up and smiled. "Could you come back tomorrow, Ms. Veterinarian? We could use your help."

Beth Ann nodded and stretched out her hand. "I would be happy to if you have animals to treat."

The nurse nodded. "We have a stable, so perhaps you could help out there. We have a man who runs it, but he's old, doesn't see well, and knows nothing about horses." She hesitated. "You see, people get jobs based on their relationship to Kim Jong-un, and this man is a distant cousin of our leader."

Beth Ann bobbed her head. "That would be fine. By the way, my name is Beth Ann Noble."

"I am Bina Chung. Nice to meet you."

"You as well."

Beth Ann returned to her quarters, happy now that she'd have something to do.

❖❖❖❖❖

A day later, Dennis Norman connected with Kim Jong-un. The dictator was delighted to host a basketball team again and thought two weeks from now would be fine. He'd have the US players compete with the DPR Korean basketball team, just like in 2013. He was especially excited when Dennis told him that Michael Forman and the others were tagging along.

While the US, South Korean, and North Korean governments authorized a charter flight from Seoul to Pyongyang, Charles Deckle coordinated with the NBA to put together a group of players and trainers, and HS supplied a South Korean to interpret. Ted Janick suggested that Jake needed to alter his appearance, so, he shaved his head and quit shaving his face. If he wore a pandemic mask and thick eyeglasses or sunglasses, no one should easily recognize him.

The day arrived to board the unmarked HS jet. The team consisted of former and current NBA players and two trainers. Jake masqueraded as a third trainer. Charles Deckle was the head coach. After a fifteen-hour flight, they landed in South Korea's Incheon Airport.

They stayed until the next day, getting over their jet lag. They then were off to Pyongyang Sunan International Airport in North Korea. Upon landing, limos took them to the Wonsan Beach Resort.

Kim Jong-un, accompanied by a group of his generals and executives, greeted them as they arrived. His entire family was there as well, including his sister Kim Yo-jong, who was rumored to be Kim Jong-un's designated successor if he were to pass.

Kim led them into a banquet room that was as large as an airport hangar. The entire group dined on traditional North Korean cuisine: beef rib soup; wild pine mushrooms; and *gajami shikhae*, a salted, fermented dish made with flounder, quinoa, garlic, and chili flakes. Kimchi and other side dishes were also served. Additionally, there was American food as well—steak, chicken, pork loin, and assorted side dishes.

The group dug in, not even thinking about how sixty percent of North Koreans had next to nothing to eat. Treavor noticed that Kim was not eating very enthusiastically, and in fact looked a bit pale and sickly.

After the meal, Kim gave the visitors a tour of the sports complex that contained the basketball court. The game was scheduled for the next day in the late afternoon.

❖❖❖❖❖

The day after visiting the clinic with the injured dog, Beth Ann Noble, accompanied by nurse Bina Chung, trekked to the stables located on the edge of the complex. It wasn't a large stable, but it was certainly magnificent. Constructed of fieldstone and expensive wood siding, it housed eight stalls for horses, all beautiful Arabians.

Sung-ho Dokgo, the stable's manager, greeted them at the entrance. He was less than five feet tall, with an olive face that looked like creased driftwood. With a gnarled cane in his right hand, he was bent over with severe scoliosis. He smiled up at Bina. "Hello, granddaughter," he said in Korean.

Bina bowed respectfully. "Hello, grandfather. This is Beth Ann Noble, a veterinarian from America."

"*Mannaseo Bangapseumnida,* Sung-ho," Beth Ann said.

He smiled cordially at Beth Ann. "Greetings," he said in English. "Please follow me." He moved slowly to a stall at the end of the stable, where he stopped and raised his cane to point at a black Arabian mare. The horse was eighteen hands high, well-muscled, with quick eyes. Her stomach was extended, and she moved toward Sung-ho for a rub on her face. He smiled as he stroked her lovingly. "*Annyeonghaseyo Aleumdaum,*" he said softly.

Bina whispered, "He just said, 'Hello, beauty.'"

Beth Ann smiled warmly as the old man turned and frowned. "She has colic, and it won't go away. We're afraid we'll have to put her down," he said in English.

Beth Ann grimaced. "I don't think it's colic."

Sung-ho shrugged. "But that's what the doctor said."

Bina turned. "Well, he didn't actually see her. When we described her bloated stomach, that's what he said."

Beth Ann frowned. "May I borrow your stethoscope?"

"Yes, of course."

"May I enter the stall?"

Sung-ho didn't respond, but opened the gate. Beth Ann entered and patted the horse on its side. "Good girl," she said quietly. She put the stethoscope on the mare's stomach and moved it around.

Beth Ann chuckled and stepped back, turning to the old man with a broad grin. "This horse doesn't have colic. She's just pregnant."

Sung-ho's eyes grew as large as dinner plates. "Pregnant? Really? Are you sure?"

Beth Ann handed him the stethoscope. "Listen for yourself. Unless she has her heart in her belly, she is, indeed, pregnant," she said with a wide smile.

Sung-ho smiled with joy. "Kim will be thrilled!"

Beth Ann cocked her head. "As in Kim Jong-un?"

"Yes, yes. This is his favorite horse."

Beth Ann's mouth curved up into a sly grin. *This just might be my ticket home!*

❖❖❖❖❖

The afternoon of the game, Beth Ann, Bina Chung, and Sung-ho were guests of honor, compliments of Kim Jong-un.

They were in the upper-level seats, midcourt, eating popcorn and sipping iced tea.

They watched the Korean national team warm up with a shoot-around. The tallest player was Kim Chol-un at 6-foot-4, but Kwang Kye, at 5-feet-11, caught Beth Ann's eye. He was launching three-point shots from everywhere and making nearly all of them. He even tried a few from just over the half-court line and made some of those.

When the US players came onto the court, she froze. Omar Carter was with the group ... not dressed to play, but with them for sure. *If Omar is here, then Jake is as well.* She scanned the rest of the group but didn't spot him.

She watched Omar standing at the end of the bench next to a bald man with a nascent beard, thick glasses, and a pandemic mask. Something about the way he moved was familiar. She thought of standing and making herself visible to Omar but decided to wait.

Once the game started, the NBA players towered over the Korean team and were much more skilled. But they weren't trying to show up the smaller Koreans, so they passed more than they needed to and didn't guard the Koreans well at all.

Then Kwang Kye entered the game, and everything changed. His first shot, a three-pointer, swished through the net, and he raised his arm with a satisfied yelp. Moments later, he did it again, then again. The US players started to guard him in earnest, but it made no difference. He simply moved farther away from the basket and made even more three-pointers. The Korean fans, including Kim Jong-un, went wild.

The smallest man on the court was thumping the NBA stars. But then Michael Forman switched off his man and began to guard Kwang like a wet blanket, and Kwang's scoring stopped.

At halftime, the people sitting behind Beth Ann left for the bathrooms and concessions. Bina took Sung-ho as well. Beth Ann looked for Omar. During the first half he had looked directly at her, so he knew she was present, but now he was nowhere in sight. That's when she heard a whisper from behind her. "Beth Ann, don't turn around."

She began to do just that, but the voice said, "Please don't. My name is Treavor Storm, and I'm with the US contingent. Jake is here, as well as Omar Carter, to take you home."

She started to turn around once more, but a hand gripped her shoulder. "I'm serious. Don't turn around."

"OK, I won't." Then she paused. "I did see Omar, but I don't see Jake."

Treavor chuckled softly. "He's the bald dude with the beard, glasses, and mask. He spotted you first. Beth Ann, do you have a room of your own?"

She bobbed her head. "Room 272 in the west wing."

"That's good. We leave midmorning tomorrow, and you'll be going with us."

Beth Ann shook her head. "I can't. I have two guards who stay near me all the time. I'm surprised they aren't here now."

"Not to worry, we have that covered." Treavor squeezed her shoulder. "Just stay in your room tomorrow morning. Don't leave, OK?"

"All right, I won't."

Then there was silence. Beth Ann turned around after a few moments but saw nothing. She trembled with excitement. *Jake is here, Omar as well, and they have friends to help. But how will they do it? Jake can't kill everyone. Is he going to kill Kim Jong-un? Oh, Lord.*

❖❖❖❖❖

The next morning, Jake, Omar, and Treavor hiked up to Beth Ann's room. A bodyguard was standing next to the door. He was short, wide, and very muscular. He had a sidearm in a shoulder holster and a scowl on his face when he saw Jake and Omar. As they approached Beth Ann's room, he turned, and his scowl deepened. "What you do here?" he asked in broken English.

"We came to visit our friend, Ms. Noble," Omar answered quickly as Jake knocked on her door.

The bodyguard drew his sidearm and pointed it at Jake just as Beth Ann opened the door. "You need leave," said the guard as he shifted the gun to Omar, who had stepped forward.

"Why? We're just visiting an old friend.".

"Leave now," said the guard forcefully as he put his finger on the trigger.

Omar shook his head. "Why do you have to be this way? It's just a quick visit," he said as he started to step toward the open door.

The guard began to squeeze the trigger, but Jake Silver pointed at him and said, "Just die." The guard collapsed to the floor as if there was no gravity.

Beth Ann brought her hand to her mouth. "Oh my God, Jake, you killed him!

"Yes, I did. There was no other way."

Omar glanced around, confirming that the hallway was empty. He bent down, grabbed the guard, and hauled him into Beth Ann's room."

Once inside, Beth Ann hugged and kissed Jake. "My God, Jake, what the heck am I doing here?" she asked.

Jake stood back. "You were abducted so I could kill more people for Kim Jong-un."

"Oh no."

"Yes, and he said if I didn't, he'd kill you."

"Holy shit, are you serious? They've been treating me so well I never thought my life was in danger. Who does he want you to kill?"

"The prime minister of Israel."

"Oh my God!"

"'Oh my God' is right. There's no way I'm doing that, so that's why we're here. The basketball game was put together quickly so we could rescue you. And now we need to leave quickly. The limos should be loading up soon."

"Okay, but who else is here? Someone spoke to me at the game, but he wouldn't let me see him."

"Ah, yes. That was another member of the crew. It will sound impossible, but he's invisible."

"Say what?"

"I'm invisible," ventured Treavor.

Beth Ann flinched.

"I'm the one who sat behind you. Treavor Storm, at your invisible service."

Jake said, "Hey, if I can point at people, say 'Just die,' and they do, why is it so difficult to understand that a man could be invisible?"

Beth Ann shook her head. "This is ... just ... a lot to swallow all at once."

Omar laughed. "No shit, but can we about it later? We need to get moving." He peered at the dead guard. "I'll stash this guy in the closet."

Jake grasped Beth Ann's shoulders. "Treavor is going to carry you, and when he does, you'll also be invisible."

Beth Ann moaned. "This just gets better and better."

"I won't pick you up until I need to, okay?" Treavor said.

"Sure, whatever," Beth Ann replied.

The group moved out into the hall, down the stairs, and onto the sidewalk. They walked about a quarter mile to the circular drive at the front of the complex, where a limo sat waiting for Jake and Omar. The other limos had already departed with the NBA players. At the edge of the last building, Treavor hoisted Beth Ann onto his shoulders as the group moved quickly toward the limousine.

Kim Jong-un was waiting there with a few of his cronies, and as Jake and Omar approached, he extended his hand. "Thanks for coming," he said in Korean. The interpreter standing next to him repeated it in English. Omar and Jake responded in kind. Luckily, Kim failed to recognize Jake when he shook his hand.

Omar opened one of the rear doors of the limo on the far side as Treavor squatted down and put Beth Ann in the car. "Get down," he whispered to her. Then he climbed in after her. Omar followed and shut the door, while Jake slipped in on the other side, exposing Beth Ann.

Kim Jong-un's face puckered as he spotted Beth Ann. He started to say something as the limo began to pull away, but Jake slid the window down, pointed a finger at Kim, and said, "Just die." Then the dictator collapsed as if he were a Korean puppet with his strings severed.

The men around him were stunned, and they all crouched down to see what had happened while the limo sped off. The driver was totally unaware of what had occurred.

Jake reached across and touched Beth Ann's arm, then whispered, "Good to see you, my love."

9

DURING THE DEBRIEFING at the White house, Jake said nothing about having killed Kim Jong-un. The North Koreans were keeping the news under wraps, though that couldn't last for long. Kim had looked sickly and haggard at the ballgame, so maybe his death would be attributed to whatever was ailing him. Besides, even if the president had his suspicions once the death was announced, Jake thought plausible deniability would be in everyone's best interests.

As they left the Oval Office, Tony Seiffer pulled Jake aside. "The president would like you and Dr. Storm back here in a bit. He has an assignment for you." He paused and grinned. "But you can have a month or so to get reacquainted with that lovely woman first." Then he winked and sent him on his way with a pat on the shoulder.

On the flight back to the Twin Cities, Beth Ann got up and sat next to Treavor. "Thank you, Dr. Storm, for rescuing me from that madman."

"I'm just glad that it worked out," Treavor responded.

"Jake told me that you helped him in a couple of assassinations for Kim."

"Yes, in Equatorial Guinea. President Nguema apparently crossed Kim Jong-un by was cozying up to the United States, so Jake eliminated him as instructed, along with his son, Teodorin. It turned out pretty well for the people of the country, since Prime Minister Botey will now run for president and make major reforms."

"Well, that's good."

"We were also supposed to murder an ex-president of South Korea, but she is now enjoying a million-dollar payoff and luxurious relocation, courtesy of the US government," Treavor said with a quiet chuckle.

Beth Ann shook her head. "It's all so crazy, but I really do appreciate what you did for me and the help you give Jake."

"My pleasure."

Beth Ann hesitated. "Jake said that your fiancée bailed on you when you became invisible."

Treavor exhaled. "Oh yes. She's got a new man now."

"I'm sorry. That must be tough."

"Well, yes and no. I was totally devastated at first, but now I'm seeing a woman named Eleanor Milburn. We met on the job, and she has no problem with me being invisible."

"That's wonderful. I would surely like to meet her."

Treavor smiled. "That can be arranged, most definitely."

❖❖❖❖❖

Two weeks later, Tony Seiffer called Jake and Treavor, telling them to come to the Oval Office the day after tomorrow at 1 p.m. A driver would pick them up from Treavor's house at 9 a.m. for the flight.

The next day, Seiffer, Treavor, and Jake strode into the famous office. Secretary of State Jill Foyberger, seated on one of the couches, was wearing a pale blue pantsuit that matched her eyes. The president up when they entered, moved toward Jake, and shook his hand. "Dr. Storm, I assume you're here. How about a shake?"

"Yes, sir, I'm here. Nice to see you again," Treavor said as he grasped the president's outstretched hand.

"Gentlemen, I'd like you to meet our secretary of state. I was just bringing her up to speed on your unique talents."

The secretary didn't rise for a handshake, just nodded at Jake with a solemn look on her face. Then she turned and watched the couch sag a bit as Treavor sat down.

"I heard about both of you before but wasn't sure I believed it until now. I'm indebted to both of you for your service to the country. You're both heroes in my book," she said with a smile.

Jake nodded and Treavor said, "Thank you."

She laughed spontaneously. "My God, Dr. Storm, you really are invisible!"

The president cleared his throat. "Listen, let's not waste time. I'm about to ask you to go on a mission that will probably take quite a while, and it's quite possible you may not return."

Jake sat forward. "What do you mean?"

"I mean it's very dangerous, and you both could be killed, even with your unique talents."

Jake sat back and took a deep breath. "Well, that doesn't sound good."

"No, I suppose not, and you don't have to accept the assignment. But let me lay it out for you. As you know, one of our biggest threats is the Islamic State and its various factions and allies. We've been killing their leaders sporadically, usually by drone strike. The problem with that is that it's often not enough, and sometimes we have civilian casualties. That's counterproductive, to say the least. Also, there are always other leaders waiting in the wings."

"I want to send both of you to the Middle East to take the fight to them at ground level. We will target as many of their leaders as possible, plus their associates and any other key players. We aim to render them ineffective once and for all," he said forcefully.

Jake spoke. "How exactly would this work, sir?"

"We have someone on the inside, a bodyguard for their current leader, a man known as Abu al-Husain al-Husaini al-Quraishi, though we believe his real name is Juma Awad al-Baderi. The bodyguard feeds us a small amount of information, and it's sporadic, but what we do know is that Abu has a laptop computer that he takes with him wherever he goes. When he's able, he signs on and sends encrypted emails. Now, we have no way of accessing those emails, so what we need you to do is slip a flash drive into his PC, then when he does sign on, we'll be able to track where his other leaders are and what they plan on doing."

"Then what?" asked Jake.

"Then you seek out them and kill them, one by one. It could take months, and you'd have to go wherever in the world they're located. Once you get them all, your last assignment will be to circle back and kill Abu."

Jake drew in a deep breath. "Wow, that's ambitious. There are so many ways it could all go wrong."

"Men, I won't lie. There's a very good chance of one or both of you could end up dead. You will have little if any support or chance of rescue. Some of these locations will be in remote mountain caves or large, hidden training grounds."

Treavor cleared his throat. "So, not quite a suicide mission, but close."

The secretary of state nodded. "Our analysts say there's a 50-50 chance that you both come back alive."

Jake's jaw tightened. "Seriously, I don't know about this one. I was planning on getting married and having kids, not dying in a damned cave."

"Amen to that!" echoed Treavor.

"I understand, and as I said at the beginning, it's strictly voluntary. Your decision," the president responded.

"Good. I don't know about Treavor, but I don't see how I can accept," Jake said.

"Sir, I understand this could put a huge crimp in the Islamic State, but I don't want to die either," Treavor added.

The president glanced at his watch. "Why don't you two get take some time and discuss it?" Then he stood up. "Let me know either way."

Everyone stood up, no one shook hands, and Jake and Treavor filed out.

❖❖❖❖❖

That evening, Treavor and Jake had room service in Jake's hotel room, even though they weren't very hungry. They were torn about what to do about the president's request. Neither wanted to die, of course, but could they pass up the chance to end the threat from the Islamic State? After going back and forth between the two, Jake's cell rang. It was Beth Ann.

"Hi, sweetheart. What's happening in the nation's capital?" she asked.

"Lots of stuff, I guess," Jake said.

"No, silly, I mean what did the president want?"

"Umm, I really don't know what to say."

"What does that mean?"

"Um ... well, he proposed a long mission to ... um ... deal with Islamic terrorists," Jake said reluctantly.

"Dammit, Jake, quit beating around the bush."

Treavor whispered, "Tell her ... see what she thinks."

Jake told Beth Ann what the president and secretary of state had proposed, word for word. When he finished, there was a long pause at the end of the line.

"Wow, Jake. Just a 50-50 chance of surviving?"

"Yeah, no kidding."

"Well, from what you said, the first mission wouldn't be terribly dangerous, right? You wouldn't need to kill anyone, just support Treavor as he downloads Abu's data."

"Actually, that's true. Let me run that by Treavor."

"OK, fine. I love you, babe. And whatever you decide, I'll love you either way."

"Thanks, sweet pea. I love you big tons."

"You better."

Jake turned to Treavor and explained Beth Ann's suggestion. Treavor thought for a minute, then said, "You know, she's right. We can do the one assignment and see what happens next. What do you think?"

"I'm in if you are, Treavor."

"All right, then. Let's call Tony Seiffer."

After they laid out their plan for the mission, Seiffer agreed it was a good idea and said he would present it to the president. Two hours later, they got the green light. They were to come in bright and early two days from now to map out the logistics, then they would be heading for Baghdad.

10

JAKE AND TREAVOR LANDED at Baghdad International Airport by way of Qatar Airways. Jake wore a white-and-red-checkered *kufiyah* and a white robe over his clothes. His passport proclaimed him to be a Palestinian by the name of Professor Jabbar Easau Danjani from Palestine University. The professor who actually did exist, but currently was taking a much-needed vacation in an Israeli jail cell.

The duo had the plane to themselves since the US government had purchased all the other seats. Jake enjoyed the undivided first-class service, while Treavor took an Ambien and slept for most of the flight.

When the plane landed, Jake moved through customs with Treavor as his shadow. They were met at the baggage claim by a tall, thin man with a hatchet face and a protruding Adam's apple. He was holding a small placard that had *Danjani* written on it. Once their luggage arrived, the man led them to a black SUV and tossed the baggage in the back.

The driver didn't say a word as he drove west and away from Baghdad to a modest home on the outskirts. He pulled into a short gravel driveway, got out, yanked the luggage out of the back, and headed to the front door. He set the baggage on the front step and left, silent as ever.

The door immediately opened, and Ted Janick stood in front of them with a shit-eating grin on his face.

"Hi, guys, welcome to Baghdad. Hot enough for you?"

Jake scooped up the luggage and walked into the air-conditioned home. "I'll say. It's gotta be at least 95 degrees."

"More like 102, but it's a dry heat," said Ted with a facetious smile. "So, did you bring your invisible sidekick with you, or did he decide to stay home?"

"I'm here," Treavor replied. "When did you get here?"

"Yesterday, and I thought you might like it if I stocked this place for you with some groceries and liquor. You aren't supposed to be able to buy booze here, but that law is pretty much ignored."

Jake smiled. "Thanks for that. A gin and tonic sounds good with this heat. Let us freshen up, then we can talk about how we're going to do this."

"Be my guest."

Afterward, they convened in the small kitchen, and Ted served up gin and tonics.

"So, what's the plan?" inquired Jake.

"Well, thankfully, Abu is still in Baghdad in a small apartment building that's occupied by his men. He has the top floor all to himself and seldom leaves. He wakes up at dawn and goes out on the patio for prayers. That's when you'll do the job."

Ted held up a key. "This is the key to the front door, supplied by our insider. When you enter, the stairs are on the left. Head up to the third floor. The laptop is normally on his desk in a small office. You'll insert a high-speed USB drive, so the download will just take a few minutes. Then you get the heck out of there. Should be a piece of cake."

Treavor snorted. "Yeah, right. We'll see about that."

"Well, I'm sure you can handle anything that comes up. Just don't kill Abu. We need him communicating with the rest of his leaders."

"Okay, how I do we get to the residence?"

"I have a car from one of our local contacts, so I'll take you, wait until you're done, then we'll head back here."

"OK, I guess that works. At least, I hope so."

❖❖❖❖❖

Dawn came early, and the sky nearly gray, with a light mist covering everything. The crew climbed into the car and sped quickly through the light traffic. Ted pointed out Abu's building, an ugly, brick structure that had seen better days. "No guards this early. I'll turn around and drop you off just down the block," he muttered.

"Roger that," Jake responded.

Ted made an illegal U-turn, almost hitting a speeding vehicle that appeared out of nowhere. He pulled up to the curb, and Jake and Treavor hopped out and looked around. There was no one visible on the street, so Treavor squatted down and lifted Jake onto his shoulders in a fireman's carry. They headed straight for the door of the apartment building.

There was a guard inside the entryway, sitting on the floor on a small mat, facing the doorway and praying. He saw the door open, apparently by itself, paused his prayers and waited for someone to enter. When no one did, he stood up and walked toward the door, picking up his battered Kalashnikov. He moved forward tentatively, the rifle in the crook of his shoulder, with a perplexed expression on his face.

Treavor slowly climbed the stairs up to Abu's floor and in through the unlocked door.

They entered a room with a small, outdated TV with rabbit ears. There was a threadbare couch and upholstered lounge chairs that looked as old as Methuselah. The floor was scarred, timeworn wood, and dust covered everything.

Treavor moved through the room and down a narrow hall that smelled like mold and fried cabbage. At the end of the hall was Abu's office, but he wasn't praying on the patio as he should've been. He was seated at his desk, working on his PC. "Son of a beach," Treavor said to himself.

Jake whispered, "Now what?"

Treavor turned to the right into a larger room. On the far wall was a patio with sliding glass doors. Against a wall rested an old bureau, and on the scarred surface sat a geometric sculpture made of stone and metal. Treavor moved toward it and picked it up. It was perfect for what he had in mind. He moved toward the glass door and tossed it through, and a resounding crash filled the room. Glass flew everywhere, and Abu came flying out of his office, just as Treavor had hoped.

As Abu hurried toward the shattered window, Treavor darted to the office and quickly inserted the flash drive into the PC.

"Good move," whispered Jake. "Aren't I getting heavy?"

Treavor chuckled. "You ain't heavy, you're my brother!"

The flash drive did its thing, and Treavor pocketed it and moved out of the office. Abu was peering out at the patio, wondering what in the world had happened.

Jake whispered, "Let's get the hell out of here." But the bodyguard stood in the doorway, blocking it.

"Oh, shit!" Treavor muttered.

Jake grunted softly, pointed, and uttered "Just die," then the man collapsed like a bag of wet towels. Jake mumbled, "Boy, I hope that wasn't our good guy bodyguard."

Treavor wasted no time, stepping over the man and scooting down the stairs, then out into the street, where he put Jake down with a groan.

"Let's find Ted," Treavor said. They moved quickly toward the prearranged rendezvous spot and pulled up short. Ted was sitting in the back of a police car. The lights on the cop car's rack lit up, and it slowly pulled away.

"Holy shit!" Jake wailed.

"Let's follow them," Treavor suggested.

Jake nodded, and they hurried to Ted's vehicle. Thankfully, the keys were still in it, so Jake started it and quickly drove off. Within four blocks, they caught up to the police car. It was moving at the designated speed limit, and

Jake tailed it at a safe distance. They went up Haifa Street for two miles, then right on Falastin, and left on Al Rasheed Street and into the police station's parking lot. Jake stopped half a block away, and they watched a handcuffed Ted being led into the back entrance to the station.

Jake shook his head. "We sure didn't plan for this."

"I'll say. I wonder what they arrested him for?"

"I have no idea, but we need to do something."

After a few moments, Treavor spoke up. "Well, I'm going in there to see what's going on. If they lock him up, we're screwed."

"All right, let's do it."

"No, Jake, you stay here. No need for you to come in and start killing a bunch of cops."

"Aw, I wouldn't do that."

Treavor grunted. "Yeah, right. Just sit tight, and I'll be back soon ... I hope."

Treavor got out of the car and headed into the police station. There was a small waiting area in the front with six plastic chairs, unoccupied at this time of the morning.

The receptionist's face was oval and leathery, and she had a hawk-like nose, dry lips, and dark, empty eyes. She was filling out a form and didn't look up as Treavor hopped over the three-foot gate. From there, he walked past four desks, only one of which was occupied by a woman typing on an old-fashioned **IBM** typewriter.

Treavor moved past her to a door that led to the back of the station. He opened the door and entered a wide room with several cubicles on the right. Officers in uniform occupied two of them—one chatting on a phone, a cup of hot tea in his hand, and the other looking closely at his computer with a frosty expression on his face.

On the left was an office that Treavor assumed housed the chief because it was huge. Although it was empty, it was cluttered with stacks of paper and green binders.

Next, Treavor went up to a room where Ted Janick sat with a sleepy-looking police officer across the table from him. Ted was talking to the officer as Treavor opened the door and scooted in, leaving the door open behind him. The officer turned, a scowl on his face, paused, then stood up and moved to the doorway. His scowl deepened as he walked into the adjoining room and barked at the officer working on the computer, who, in turn, barked back at him. No love lost between them.

Treavor moved quickly toward Ted and whispered, "Ted, it's me. Stand up, and I'll get you the heck out of here."

Ted froze for a moment, then stood up. "Step back, Ted, and I'll pick you up," Treavor said softly. He squatted down and hoisted him up and across his shoulders with a grunt. "Man, Ted, have you gained weight?" he whispered.

Ted chuckled quietly. "Muscle, Treavor, just muscle."

The police officer walked back into the room. He puckered his lips, and his eyebrows knit. Yelling in Arabic, he dashed out the door toward the front of the building.

Treavor moved toward the conference room door and started to follow him, but Ted whispered, "Turn around. We came in from the back."

"Roger that," replied Treavor.

They headed to the back of the police station and out the door. There were cop cars in the back lot and a few civilian cars as well. Treavor turned left and hiked around the building to the street.

The officer was scrambling back toward the station, mumbling to himself and obviously pissed off. He stopped at the front door and scanned the street for Ted. He sighed disgustedly and went back into the station.

Treavor walked to Ted's car, huffing and puffing as he went. When he got there, he slid Ted off his shoulders and glanced at Ted's fat stomach. "Muscle, my ass. Lay off the cheeseburgers, Teddy," he joked.

Ted laughed and opened the back door of the vehicle. "Let's get the fuck out of here, quick!"

They sped off as Baghdad was coming to life, cars and buses filling the streets in a classic morning rush hour. Ted explained what had happened. "Apparently, my U-turn was witnessed by the police officer who was interviewing me in the station. Turns out, this car was stolen. Can you believe it?"

Jake and Treavor groaned.

"Yeah, I know, so they were going to book me for stealing the car. Thank God you pulled me out of there!"

"You bet. I assume you had a fake ID with you?"

"Actually, I used yours."

"Very funny," Treavor replied.

"Of course I used a fake ID. Don't be dumb." Ted paused. "So, how did it go at Abu's place?"

"Not as expected. Abu was working on the computer and I had to distract him by breaking a window. Then Jake had to kill a bodyguard so we could get out of there. But I did get what we came for."

"Well, that's what counts. Nice work, thinking on your feet like that."

"Yeah, I thought so, too. So, now what?"

"We head back to the house, lose this car, then I'll arrange for us to get picked up this afternoon."

"OK. I can't wait to get out of here."

"Me too."

❖❖❖❖❖

Two days later, they were back in the secretary of state's office with a young man named Raj Murty. Raj had a PhD in computer science from Stanford University and was as smart as a whip. He had easily decrypted the files from Abu's computer and was explaining what they had learned.

"Abu has given a man known as Abdul Mohammad Al-Nobari an important assignment. We don't have Abdul's photo, but we know that he has a scar that runs from his forehead to his chin. Abdul is to fly to London and rendezvous with a group of ISIS cohorts. They plan to blow up Westminster Abbey while the royal family is attending services. The main target is Queen Elizabeth II. The queen has been notified, but as usual, she dismissed the threat. Her reaction was that she had served her country for seventy years, and that if she took every proposed threat to her safety seriously, she'd never go out in public."

Scotland Yard and the London police had been notified, and were already aware that several potential Islamic State cells had assimilated into London's Muslim population. Their agents had been keeping an eye on the most obvious persons of interest, but they weren't wanted men, so they weren't in custody. They were spread out, across the city, and it just wasn't feasible to watch all of them constantly.

11

TREAVOR AND JAKE'S jet landed at Heathrow Airport. They were met by Assistant Commissioner Oscar J. Wilson and a few of his lesser cohorts. Oscar was of average height with a clean-shaven unremarkable face, a gruff smoker's voice, and a flinty personality. He walked them past customs with a flash of his badge and into a waiting limousine. He climbed into the passenger seat while Jake, Ted, and the unannounced Treavor got into the bench back seat.

Wilson turned to Ted and Jake. "I know you must be knackered from the flight over, so we'll take you to your hotel and let you get some rest. We'll pick you up in the morning and have a bit of a chat. By the way, the hotel room is compliments of Scotland Yard, but food and drinks are on your tab."

They were driven to the Sloane Square Hotel, formerly known as the Royal Court. The driver was a young officer who introduced herself as Olivia Brown. She had a lovely face, short red hair, and freckles on her nose. She turned around to them as she pulled up to the front of the hotel. "I'll pick you up at 9 a.m. tomorrow. The hotel restaurant is quite good. Try the fish and chips at the BrewDog IPA." She flashed a quick smile and drove off.

Ted sighed as he looked at Olivia's vehicle speeding away. "My God, I think I'm in love."

Jake chuckled. "She's attractive, I'll give you that. Come on, I'm hungry."

They checked in without going to their rooms and headed to the restaurant, where they all enjoyed the recommended fish and chips and the ale as well.

The next morning, they enjoyed a delightful breakfast dubbed a *fry up*. It included fried eggs, sausage, back bacon, tomatoes, mushrooms, fried bread, and a small cup of black pudding. It was delicious and consumed with minimal chatter.

At 9 a.m., they were huddled in front of the hotel. It was raining lightly from a pale-blue sky. Officer Brown pulled up next to them under the hotel's protective overhang. Ted climbed into the front seat, and the invisible Treavor slid into the back with Jake.

"Good morning, gents. How are you today?" she asked pleasantly.

"We're fine, rested, full of food, and ready to do what we came here for," Ted said emphatically.

Olivia pulled away and said nothing, then drove all the way to the eight-story Scotland Yard building in Westminster. She parked, and they all trooped inside and were screened. They got into an elevator and headed up to the top floor. There, she escorted them to a conference room that could have hosted a small army. There was bottled water, coffee, and the requisite tea on a sideboard with assorted scones and crumpets. Treavor dearly wanted a cup of coffee, but resisted the urge because he wasn't supposed to be in attendance. Ted took a bottle of water, and they sat down and waited. Olivia made a cup of Earl Grey tea, adding milk and a lump of sugar.

After a few minutes, the conference room door opened, and Oscar J. entered first, followed by three of his assistants. He sat at the head of the table and looked at Jake and Ted.

"You appear well-rested today. I must say, the older I get, the more tiresome jet lag gets. Did you know that the hotel you're staying in was the Beatles' favorite?" he asked.

Jake grunted. "Yes, the zillion autographed photos in the bar pretty much gave it away."

"Ah yes, indeed. I never cared much for the band. I'm more of a classical music fan," Oscar replied.

Ted answered pleasantly, "I'm an Eagles fan myself."

Oscar frowned. "As in the bird or the football team?"

Ted laughed. "Never mind, it's not important. So, what can you tell me about our joint mission?"

Oscar leaned forward. "Well, gentlemen, it seems that our commissioner received a call from your secretary of state, and you'll be allowed inside the church on Sunday. Just as bystanders, though. You won't be armed and won't interfere if something should transpire," he stated firmly. "I know you Yank cowboys like to run everything, but this is still Scotland Yard's operation. I am understood, gentlemen?"

Ted responded, "Oh, we understand—no guns, knives, or hatchets," he said, chuckling softly.

Oscar scowled. "This is not a laughing matter, sir. We don't expect anything to happen on Sunday. This kind of rumor is all too common and normally much ado about nothing. However, we've had two officers in the church around the clock since we first heard of this so-called plot, watching for anyone suspicious. So far, nothing, but we'll continue to be vigilant. This is, as you say in the States, 'not our first rodeo.'"

Jake leaned toward Ted and whispered, "I just hope he doesn't get bucked off."

❖❖❖❖❖

Treavor arose Sunday morning and ran for three miles in the morning mist, curtailing his usual distance. He had an ominous feeling about today. After the run, he showered, got dressed, then headed to the café where he sat down to eat with Ted and Jake. However, he had no appetite, so he settled for coffee and mulling.

After the meal, they all moved to the front of the hotel and watched as Olivia pulled up to the hotel. On the drive to Westminster Abbey, the men admired the London architecture. There were many brand-new buildings mixed with older brick structures, a few looking like they had made it through World War II. Olivia parked in the lot across the street from the abbey, which was nearly empty. The service wasn't going to start for another hour.

"Follow me, gents. I'll give you the tour," Olivia offered.

The abbey was more than impressive. It wasn't just a cathedral, but more like a college campus, with building after spectacular building, many connected in the center by a 50-by-50-foot green lawn that ran along a wide, brick sidewalk. The lawn was wet and uninviting, but greener than a dollar bill. On a rare sunny day, it would be very inviting.

Inside the multi-steepled cathedral, the ceiling rose to the heavens. The altar was incredibly ornate, and the numerous stained-glass windows paid tribute to the saints, the Apostles, and the Lord Himself.

A section in the front reserved for the royal family was separated by purple velvet ropes. Two officers were leading bomb-sniffing dogs up and down the pews. Uniformed officers were positioned strategically, their faces void of expression. Olivia walked the men up the stairs to one of the immense bell towers. The huge bells were polished and ready to chime with ear-crushing reverberations. Everyone was grateful they were not pealing at the moment.

They finished the lengthy tour as the cathedral was beginning to fill up. Altar boys with white surplices over black cassocks scurried on and around the altar, lighting candles. Olivia led the way to the back pew and indicated that they should sit there. Treavor ignored her and began walking up and down the aisles, checking out the parishioners. He was searching for someone with a long scar or who looked jittery and out of place, but saw no one like that. He returned to the back pew just as the royal family came out from the front of the church and took their designated seats.

The parishioners buzzed as they entered, with lots of nods and smiles of approval. The rear of the church filled up, standing room only, then the doors were closed and the service began. Treavor turned around to scan the new arrivals. They all seemed like ordinary churchgoers, mostly elderly, with a few tourists. Treavor was about to turn back when he spotted a man and a short woman in a black frock who appeared to be extremely thick through her stomach and chest. He looked closer and saw that the man had a long scar from his forehead that disappeared into his beard. *Abdul.*

Treavor tapped Jake's arm. "Guess who just showed up?"

Jake cocked his head. "Who?"

"Abdul, and he's with and a woman whose body doesn't match her face. I'm guessing she's wearing a vest loaded with explosives, but I could be wrong."

Jake began to turn around, but Treavor stopped him. "Don't turn around. I don't want you to spook them."

"Okay. Should we let Olivia know?"

Treavor sucked in a deep breath. "No, not yet. I'm going back there to make sure I'm right first. Stay put."

He stood and sauntered back to Abdul and the woman. As he got within a few feet, he saw that the woman appeared to be drugged and smelled like lemons. He remembered reading that lemon scent can throw off bomb-sniffing dogs. The small woman was sweating profusely, and her hand gripped something with a button on the top. Abdul whispered to her and pointed at the royal family, then took off.

Treavor slid into Abdul's spot. The woman was praying to herself, on the verge of panic. Then she began to count, backward. Treavor then realized that she was giving Abdul enough time to get away before detonating her payload. It was now or never, so Treavor reached over, stuck two fingers in her sweaty hand, and pulled. The detonator slipped to the middle of her hand, and she gasped. Treavor wrapped the rest of his fingers around her hand and yanked. The device fell to the floor as the woman whimpered, then fainted. Treavor dropped to the floor with her, grabbed the collar of her frock, and ripped it open. And there it was ... enough explosives to destroy the entire cathedral.

He glanced up, and Ted and Olivia were standing over him as Bobbies and plainclothesmen rushed the parishioners out of the cathedral. The royal family had been evacuated at the first sign of trouble.

Ted smiled. "Nice job, Treavor."

Olivia grunted. "Who the hell are you talking to?"

Ted laughed. "Just my invisible buddy, Dr. Treavor Storm. I'll introduce you later. Right now, you'd better call a bomb squad here to defuse this, pronto!"

While Treavor was busy saving the queen and everyone in the cathedral, Jake went after Abdul. Jake stood on the steps and spotted Abdul moving at a hurried pace toward a parked car with three men in it. Jake broke into a mad dash and was within shouting distance from Abdul. As the terrorist began to open the front passenger door, Jake called out, "Hey, you forgot something,!" Abdul stopped and turned with a perplexed look on his face. Jake pointed at Abdul and screamed, "You forgot to 'just die'!"

The men in the car were stunned as Abdul dropped to the sidewalk. A car door opened and a man emerged as Jake got close to the vehicle. "Hey you, 'just die,'" Jake said flatly, and the man collapsed as if there was no gravity. Jake bent down and pointed at the other men in the car. One pointed a handgun at Jake's chest, and Jake dropped to the ground as a slug whizzed over the spot where he had been standing a second ago. Jake pointed and repeated his deadly phrase, and the man followed his cohorts to hell. The driver, having seen enough, pulled out into the street and drove off, unscathed.

Jake rolled over and grinned as light rain speckled his face. *Hey, three out of four ain't bad.*

❖❖❖❖❖

It was late Sunday afternoon, and Olivia, Ted, Jake, and Treavor were in the office of Scotland Yard's top dog, Commissioner Henry S. Smith, commonly called Hess. He sported a gleaming gold badge with a crown, a pip, and a commander's symbol. Oscar Wilson was there as well, a bit subdued from having been taken to the woodshed for his reluctance to include the Americans from the beginning.

After he introduced himself and expressed his gratitude, Hess glanced at Oscar, then at Jake. "The woman with the explosive vest is talking extensively. She and her family are from Syria and have been here for about two years. Unfortunately, they became a target for our terrorists because they have very little money. Her name is Faiza Abdula, and the Islamic State is providing support for the entire family— but only if Faiza gives up her life. If she refused, they would kill her children and her parents. These men are animals and need to be stopped."

Hess said, "Gentleman, your secretary of state has explained how your government has been using your special abilities. I must say I still don't understand the half of it. Could you tell me how in the world you gained these powers?"

Hess listened in fascination as Treavor told him about the frigid day he became invisible, and how anything or anyone he picks up will also disappear. "My man, I'm simply gobsmacked! That's the most incredible tale I've ever heard. And you, Mr. Silver, have the power to point at people, say 'Just die,' and they do?"

"Yes, sir," Jake replied, and explained how he had gained his lethal ability after a sudden stroke.

"Crikey, that's just beyond belief. And now the two of you are working together as agents of your Homeland Security agency? Extraordinary! Do you think you could work your magic for us?"

"I'm not sure it's magic ... more like extermination of some nasty people," Jake responded.

"Bloody hell, that's good. Exterminator. Just the word for you and that damned German, Arnold Schwarzenegger," he said with a muted chuckle.

Treavor chimed in. "Actually, that would be 'terminator'."

Hess nodded. "Even better, you're terminators. I think I'll see if we can borrow you for a week or so. Perhaps you can finish what you started here."

Jake shrugged. "That's not my decision, but our president has us on a mission to break up the Islamic State, and we're just getting started."

Hess turned and contemplated Oscar, who was sulking, his scowl firmly in place. "Listen, Oscar, I didn't mean to throw a wobbly, but you really should have included these talented blokes from the beginning. Now why don't you make amends and take them to the Duck & Waffle—on us, of course."

Oscar's scowl began to fade. "Yes, sir. Thank you, sir."

The commissioner eyed Jake. "It's the best restaurant in London, as far as I'm concerned. I wish I could join you, but I need to talk to your secretary of state and have her pave the way for your extended stay."

He smiled at Oscar. "Oscar, have a few pints and loosen up." Then he peered back at Jake. "Oscar is quite a different bloke with a few in his belly. He tells some smashing jokes when he's pissed."

Oscar nearly smiled, but said nothing.

❖❖❖❖❖

That evening, Oscar, Olivia, Jake, Ted, and Treavor took the elevator up to the top floor of the Heron Tower in London's financial sector, which housed the Duck & Waffle restaurant. The view was spectacular, with London spread out in front of them, the night lights glistening endlessly for miles and miles. Below them, the Thames River rushed toward the North Sea.

The restaurant was open day and night, serving breakfast around the clock. The group sat at a table next to the window and watched rain so light it was like falling dew. A thin waiter appeared and asked whether they would like a cocktail.

Olivia ordered Calvados, a brandy made of apples and pears made in Normandy. Ted ordered a vodka gimlet, Jake a BrewDog IPA, Oscar a pint of Guinness Stout, and Treavor whispered to Jake that he'd like a Coke.

Olivia gazed at the view as she spoke to Ted. "Isn't it beautiful?" Ted grinned and looked fondly at Olivia. Actually, more than fondly. Olivia turned and smiled, knowing full well what Ted was feeling. She felt it as well. She blushed and said, "The food here is excellent. I especially like their rack of lamb with cherry sauce. Also, they have wonderful appetizers. The maple-sriracha 'devils on horseback' are bacon-wrapped figs with a touch of extra-strong blue cheese. They also offer bacon-wrapped oysters, a dish called 'angels on horseback.' And of course, they have a London favorite, Welsh rarebit, in bite-size portions, as well as the traditional prawn cocktail," she said enthusiastically.

Just then, the waiter returned with their drinks and menus tucked smartly under his armpit. He set the cocktails down with a flourish, saving the Coke for last with a puzzled expression on his face as he looked at Jake. "Is this for you as well, sir?" he inquired.

Jake shook his head as he sipped his BrewDog. "Nope, it's for my invisible friend here." He tapped the spot in front of Treavor's chair. The server's eyebrows knitted together, then he set the glass of Coke down as instructed.

Treavor spoke. "Thank you, sir, but could I also get a glass of ice please?"

The waiter froze, inhaled half of the room's air, and slowly let it out. "Of course, sir, coming right up." He passed out the menus, laying the last one in front of Treavor's chair.

It vanished as Treavor said, "Thank you."

The waiter cocked his head, his eyes wide as dinner plates. "Is this some sort of a joke?"

Olivia spoke up. "Not at all. The good doctor is invisible, and he really doesn't get out much, so take good care of him."

The waiter shivered. "Absolutely, ma'am."

"Excellent," Olivia responded, then ordered a full round of appetizers for the table. "Please bring a prawn cocktail for each of us first," she added.

"Yes, ma'am, coming right up," he responded, then turned and hurried away, shaking his narrow head.

Olivia chuckled. "Bloody hell, that was fun. The man looked like he was going to faint when Treavor's bottle of Coke disappeared."

Everyone laughed, then pored over their menus as they sipped their beverages. Olivia continued to chuckle quietly as Oscar finished his first Guinness.

❖❖❖❖❖

At the end of the meal, Oscar, having consumed three or more pints, started to tell jokes. Before that, he had Coquilles Saint-Jacques for his main course and enough appetizers to feed a platoon.

Oscar turned toward Treavor's seat. "So, Mr. Invisible, a penguin walks into a pub and jumps up on a stool at the bar. He says to the barkeep, 'Have you seen my brother in here recently?'

"The bartender puts out a lip and answers, 'I don't know. What does he look like?'" Then he laughed, while the listeners moaned.

Then he turned to Ted. "A polar bear walks into a pub and orders a pint of Guinness. The barkeep says, 'That will be twenty pounds sterling, please.' The polar bear pays and takes a seat, then the barkeep says, 'Man, this is exciting. We don't get many polar bears in here.'

"The bear looks up and replies, 'I'm not surprised, with Guinness at twenty pounds a pint.'"

The joke drew a mixture of groans and laughter.

Jake spoke up. "My turn. So, there was a small, upscale pub in New York City. It was midafternoon, and there was a Midwesterner in town early for a convention. He walked through the tavern door when the door slammed behind him. He cringed as he ambled down to the far end of the bar. There were only two other customers in the place, both sitting next to each other with their heads down on the bar, asleep until the slamming of the door woke them up. The bartender sauntered down to the new customer and asked what he'd like. 'How about a bottle of Budweiser?' the man replied. The bartender fetched it, then put it down in front of the man.

"Just then, the two blurry-eyed customers started to chat. One said to the other, 'Well, hello there, sir. How would you like me to buy you a drink?'

"The other gent straightened up with a bit of an effort. 'Why, that would be kind of you, sir.' As they sipped their beers, the second man contemplated the first man. 'Say, fellow, where are you from?'

"The first man took a long drink, burped, and answered, 'I'm originally from Dublin, Ireland.'

"The second man slapped the bar with astonishment. 'By God, I was raised in Dublin as well!' he said, grinning drunkenly. 'Let me buy the next round.'

"The first man crooked his head and asked, 'Well, if you're from Dublin, where did you go to school?'

"The second man responded, 'I went to St. Mary's.'

"The first man slapped his leg. 'By God, I did as well!'

"The new customer was now getting his second Budweiser when he eyeballed the barkeep. 'So, what's going on?' he asked as he peered at the drunken men.

"Aw, nothing," the barkeep said, grinning. "The O'Malley twins are drunk again," he replied.

Then the table roared with laughter.

12

THE NEXT MORNING, the crew gathered in Hess' office. He was puffing on a Royal Meerschaum pipe with an engraved bowl and a thin stem. The air smelled of cherry tobacco, and Hess had a welcoming smile on his face as he sat in his plush leather desk chair and waved the crew in. "How was the food at the Duck & Waffle?"

Olivia answered, "It was wonderful. I had the rack of lamb with cherry sauce, and it was scrumptious."

"Good, good," Hess replied, and he turned to his American guests. "Did you enjoy the food as well?"

Jake replied for all of them. "Very much so, and thank you. I've never had a bacon-wrapped fig with blue cheese. They were delectable."

Hess blew a stream of smoke at the ceiling and made a face. "I can't say that I've ever tried them. I don't care for figs or blue cheese. I do love bacon, though."

Treavor spoke up. "Who doesn't?"

"Indeed. I assume that was you speaking, Dr. Storm?"

"Yes, sir."

"Well, I talked to your secretary of state, and she talked to your president, and we're all agreed. You are instructed to terminate all the terrorists you can for us."

Treavor spoke. "So, what's the plan?"

Hess blew a series of smoke rings at the high celling, then placed the pipe in an ancient wooden ashtray that was scarred and burned. "Mrs. Abdula will lead you to the apartment complex where the terrorists outfitted her with the explosive vest. She doesn't know the apartment address, number, or floor, but she'll know once she sees it. As soon as she points it out, we will whisk her away. Then, Jake and Treavor, you'll do what you do best—terminate."

Jake shook his head. "What do you need us for? Why can't you storm the place and kill them yourselves?"

Hess nodded. "Because Faiza Abdula has indicated that there are young children and women in the apartment. It's large, with numerous bedrooms and such, so we don't want to go in with guns blazing and kill the innocents."

Jake nodded. "OK, that makes sense. When do we do it?"

Hess looked at the clock. "In two hours, right at lunchtime. So grab a quick bite and we'll take you to them. We will have two dozen officers surrounding the place, just in case."

Hess picked up his pipe and pointed the stem at Jake. "I appreciate this. Do your best, but call it off if things take a bad turn. We know where they are. They aren't going anywhere."

"Roger that," Jake replied, then left with the crew.

❖❖❖❖❖

The crew, along with Faiza Abdula, headed to the hamlet of Croydon. It was one of the poorest hamlets in London. Crime was rampant there, and gangs roamed the streets at all hours.

They coasted past the apartment building that Faiza had identified. It was next to a junk dealer, a rag merchant, and a boarded-up tire merchant. The faded yellow brick apartment rose out of the earth like a sore thumb. The mortar was in dire need of tuckpointing, and numerous windows were cracked. The landscaping in front of the building comprised dead English yew and scraggly hornbeam. Not a blade of grass could be seen, just bare dirt and trash.

The apartment building was three stories tall. Faiza pointed at a third level window with a black sheet for a curtain.

"That's the room where they have the explosives," Faiza said. Oscar nodded and spoke into the microphone clipped to his uniform, alerting the officers who were surrounding the building. They drove on for a block, then stopped and clambered out of the unmarked vehicle. Olivia remained with the vehicle, and the rest, including Oscar, hiked back toward the beat-up apartment building, up the cracked, concrete stairs in front, leading to the weathered front doors.

The doors were unlocked, so they entered the building. Jake went up the stairs, followed by Ted, Treavor, then Oscar and Faiza. The stairs smelled of urine, vomit, and mold.

They ascended to the top floor. Halfway down the hall, Faiza stopped in front of a scarred door. She whispered to Oscar, "This is it." Then she knocked unexpectedly. Oscar started to reach for her, but Faiza shook him off as the door opened. A man stood in the door, armed with a Sten gun--a lightweight, British submachine gun--pointed right at Faiza, who started to speak to the man. "You son of a bitch," she said in perfect English.

Jake recognized the man as the driver of the getaway car from the day before. He was of medium height, with a light-brown complexion and a face like a frying pan. He frowned as he recognized Faiza, then raised the Sten toward her chest with evil intent.

Jake wasted no time. "Just die," he barked out, and the terrorist did just that, crumbling to the ground with a loud thud. Oscar then grabbed Faiza by the arm and yanked her away, and they headed back down the stairway. Ted stood to the side and pulled out his Glock 19X as Treavor slid up behind Jake.

"I'm right behind you, Jake. Climb on my back," Treavor directed, and he gripped Jake's left arm. Jake clumsily hoisted himself up and disappeared.

Treavor stepped on the back of the dead terrorist, moved into the apartment and into the kitchen. There were five men sitting at a table, cleaning their guns. Two stood up as Treavor and Jake entered.

Jake pointed and screamed "Just die." Then again, again, again, and once more. The two men who were standing fell on the wooden floor with a thud, like a sack of wet towels. One seated terrorist slumped forward onto the machine gun he was cleaning. Another flopped to the left, but was held in place by the arms of the chair. The last terrorist slid down, whacking his forehead on the lip of the table.

Treavor grunted and turned as a door opened in the hallway. A man came out of the far room—the one with the black sheet for a curtain. Jake started to point for a "Just die" kill, but stopped. The man looked different from the rest. He was not only Caucasian, but also nearly an albino. He had enormous, jug ears that looked like he could fly like Dumbo with a strong wind. A woman appeared right behind him, clad in a vest that was loaded with explosives. The albino looked at the dead man in the open doorway and gasped. "Bloody hell, what the fuck!" he exclaimed.

The woman stared at the dead man as well, forced a quick smile, and muttered, "Good." The albino turned, slapped her in the face, and pushed her back into the room.

Treavor and Jake quickly moved to the back room and peered in. The albino and the woman were on the floor, wrestling, each gripping the explosives' detonator. It looked like she wanted to set the vest off, and he was trying to prevent that, though maybe it was the other way around. Jake pointed his finger at the albino, but the two of them were rolling and thrashing around so much he thought he might kill the woman by mistake.

Treavor decided it was time to go and leave these two to their fate. He turned and rushed past the dead men at the table, stepping once again on the back of the man in the front doorway. Ted was in the hall and Treavor yelled to him, "Get the heck out of here, Ted!" as Treavor and Jake went down the smelly stairs in a panicked rush. Ted hesitated and saw a group of women and children gathered at the end of the apartment's hallway. A young lad raised a Sten gun and pointed it at Ted, who quickly moved out of the doorway. He began to scamper down the stairs when the top floor of the building exploded with a thunderous roar.

Out in the street, Jake was still on Treavor's back when the top of the apartment building exploded. A piece of brick whacked the back of Jake's head while Treavor kept on running. Olivia was standing in the street with wide eyes, her service revolver in her hand. Treavor, covered in concrete dust, put his trembling hands on the trunk of her car. Jake moaned and collapsed to the street, now visible. The back of his head was bleeding profusely, coating the back of his shirt. Treavor crouched next to his friend, stripped off his own shirt, and pressed it to the head wound. He glanced up at Olivia, who was searching for Ted Janick. "Call an ambulance," Treavor screamed.

Olivia dialed 9-9-9, reporting an officer down and multiple casualties. She squatted next to Jake. "What happened?"

"A freakin' explosion, that's what. A woman with an explosive vest was wrestling with one of the men in the house. I'm not sure which one wanted the vest to go off, but it obviously did."

Olivia stood and peered at the burning apartment building with a look of terror on her face. People were streaming out of the first-floor doors with looks of shock and dismay on their faces. Police officers were quickly moving them away from the burning building once they stepped out into the street. A plethora of wailing sirens echoed throughout the neighborhood. The street was littered with bricks, as well as pieces of the roof, windows, and doors. And human limbs.

"Where's Ted?" Olivia whispered.

Treavor Storm, still squatting next to Jake Silver, turned and stared at the burning apartment building. "I don't know. He should have been right behind us."

Olivia shook her head. "No, he wasn't. He didn't come out the front door. I was watching."

Treavor sighed and shook his head as Jake moaned. "Then I'm afraid he didn't make it."

Olivia whimpered just as the ambulance came into view, red-and-white lights flashing and siren wailing. Olivia waved at it, and it turned and it pulled up next to her car. Two paramedics got out and quickly moved toward Jake. One bumped into Treavor and yelped.

"I'm sorry," Treavor said, and got out of the way.

The paramedic grimaced and shook his head, not knowing what he had collided with, but squatted down and focused his attention on Jake. He removed Treavor's blood-soaked shirt from the back of Jake's head, then opened a white kit with a medical symbol on it and removed a compress with adhesive on the edges. He pushed it firmly in place on the back of Jake's head, then turned to his partner and said, "The wound isn't too bad, but we need the lightweight gurney."

The partner opened the back of the ambulance and got in, then quickly emerged with the stretcher. It was lightweight, made of orange canvas, and had no wheels attached. The paramedic unfurled it and set it next to Jake. The men gingerly lifted a groaning Jake onto the gurney and loaded him into the back of the ambulance. After strapping him down, they busied themselves with checking Jake's vital signs and put an oxygen mask on him.

The driver got out and started to close the back doors of the ambulance. Treavor put his hand on it, stopping it for a second, then slid into the vehicle. Two minutes later, the ambulance headed out to the hospital, lights and siren wailing, with an invisible man in the back.

Olivia gazed at the apartment building, which was now totally engulfed in flames. Four fire engines were dousing it with water, but it continued to burn, the first and second-floor bricks glowing with the inferno's heat.

Olivia moaned once more. She whispered, "Ted," as her green eyes filled with tears.

❖❖❖❖❖

Later that evening, Treavor, Olivia, and Oscar sat in Hess' office. He wasn't happy.

"My God, what a bloody mess! Three police officers injured, one fatally, Ted Janick lost in the explosion, and we're still assessing the civilian deaths and injuries." He paused and looked at Olivia. "How is Mr. Silver doing?"

"He's going to be fine, they think. He was hit in the back of his head by a piece of a brick and may have a concussion. They're keeping him overnight again for observation."

"Well, that's a relief. If he were killed, it would put our relationship with your president in jeopardy."

No one said anything as Hess stood up and went to the window. "I've updated the secretary of state on what happened. She'd like Jake and Dr. Storm to fly back to Washington when Jake is cleared for travel."

Jake spoke again. "That's good. I think I need to reassess my options. This wasn't what I expected."

"Yes, I concur. I bloody well concur."

❖❖❖❖❖

Three days later, Treavor and Jake landed at Dulles International Airport. Jake did have a concussion, and his head wound was painful, but not life-threatening.

That afternoon, they were in the office of Secretary of State Jill Foyberger. Da Boss was there as well. Jake and Treavor had spent the last hour giving them a blow-by-blow of what happened in London. Da Boss hung his head and shook it slowly. "I wonder why Ted didn't follow you out?"

Treavor replied, "I guess we'll never know."

"Well, he was a heck of an agent, a good man, and I considered him a friend. I'll miss him very much. We're going to have a small funeral at the end of the week, even though we have nothing to bury. We're flying his father and a few close friends in for it."

Foyberger nodded. "I had only met him a few times, but I agree. He was smart and dedicated from what I could see." Then she looked at Jake and the chair that Treavor was sitting in. "Men, the president would like you to take some time off and recuperate a bit before you get back in the hunt."

Jake grunted. "I'm not sure about that. I damn near got killed, and in all honesty, killing those men just left a bad taste in my gut. I need to rethink this whole 'Just die' power. Just get married and live a normal life."

"I understand. I wouldn't want to be in your shoes. Take all the time you need to make your mind up. And should you decide to quit, you should know how grateful all of us are for all that you've done."

Then she turned to Treavor. "And you as well, Dr. Storm. You're both American heroes."

Jake and Treavor sighed.

❖❖❖❖❖

A few days later, Ted Janick's funeral was held at Arlington National Cemetery. Before becoming a Homeland Security agent, Ted had served in the US Coast Guard with distinction.

Ted Janick Sr., Ted's father, was there. Olivia flew in for the funeral, as well as Omar Carter. Da Boss was there along with a phalanx of HS agents and employees. Ted's former commanding officer from the Coast Guard was also there, along with several of Ted's buddies.

The sun was as golden as a bluebird's breast, and the sky was peppered with white clouds that looked like giant cotton balls. Since no remains could be recovered, there was no casket, just a white cross to join the 400,000 others.

The deacon was a tall, gray-haired gentleman with a warm smile. He spoke with a smooth, gentle voice. "I never had a chance to meet Ted, and I regret that I didn't. From what I'm told by his father and friends, he was a special man, and a man whom the good Lord will welcome with open arms. But here on Earth, he'll be missed by many.

"Ted Janick Jr. was smart, loyal, and very dedicated to whatever task he was performing. While he never married, I'm told that he was married to his job—first as a lieutenant commander in the Coast Guard, then as an outstanding Homeland Security agent. I hear that he was a good friend to have and was generous to a fault. His last will and testament dictated that all of his wealth will be donated to the American Red Cross."

The deacon paused and smiled warmly at the mourners. "Yes, I'm sorry that I didn't meet young Ted here, but I'll surely look him up when I finally get to Heaven. And now I have a few requests from men who knew Ted and would like to speak to you about him."

A man in a US Coast Guard admiral's uniform moved forward gracefully. He had a weathered, handsome face and dark eyes that seemed to look right through you as he turned his head and scanned those in attendance. His deep voice filled the cemetery as the sun grew brighter.

"Let me tell you a story about the young Ted Janick when he was with me in Miami. It was a year of numerous hurricanes, and folks grew weary of the constant on-again, off-again orders to evacuate. I was off duty, and Ted and three of our men were manning the station when a fishing boat alerted him that they had passed a large boat filled with Cubans headed for the coast of Florida. Their sail was snapped in half, and they were floundering while the latest hurricane was bearing down on them. The winds were up to 125 miles an hour, and it was nearly dusk when Ted roused his ensigns and set sail, armed with the coordinates that the fishing boat had provided and absolute faith in his mission. I'm told that the swells were ten to twelve feet, some cresting as high as eighteen. But intrepid Ted and his men were not deterred."

"To make this brief, Ted and his men rescued the Cubans, including eight children, two of them infants, and brought them all back safely. That, my friends, was the kind of man Ted Janick Jr. was."

The admiral lowered his head and said a quiet prayer, made a sign of the cross, looked up at the heavens, then turned and returned to the rest of the mourners. No one else spoke. The admiral had said it all.

◆◆◆◆◆

That evening, many of the funeral guests gathered at Da Love of Soul, a restaurant frequented by Homeland Security. They sat in a room in the back, celebrating the life of Ted Janick Jr. Olivia had changed from her black funeral garb into a lovely lemon-yellow blouse and pearl-gray pants. A modest string of pearls hung from her neck, complemented by pearl earrings. She looked fabulous, but very, very sad.

Jake took Olivia by the arm and introduced her to Ted's father. Ted Sr. shook her hand. "I understand you're with Scotland Yard and made the trip just for my son's funeral."

Olivia nodded. "I did. I only knew Ted Jr. for a few days, but from the moment I met him, I could tell what a special human being he was."

Ted Sr. smiled and sighed. "He was, indeed. I can't fathom that he's gone."

Jake turned toward Olivia. "Ted would really appreciate you being here. The first time Ted saw you in London, he immediately said that he was in love."

Olivia's eyes widened. "Really?"

"Oh yes, absolutely."

Ted Sr. chimed in. "Well, that's just wonderful. He must have seen something very special in you. As you know, he was married to his job."

"I don't know about that, but I felt an immediate attraction to him too." She paused and wiped away a tear. "I was really hoping to get to know him better."

Ted Sr. took her hand. "It sounds like Ted would've liked that very much."

Olivia smiled shyly. "May I give you a hug?"

Ted Sr.'s face brightened. "Oh, please do."

And she did ... for a long time ... as they both wept silently.

❖❖❖❖❖

The next day, Treavor and Jake were back at Dulles International Airport. They would be boarding a Homeland Security plane back to Minneapolis in a half hour. Jake was checking the weather back home when his cell phone chimed. It was Tony Seiffer, the president's chief of staff, with a request that the two of them come to the White House later that afternoon.

Jake shook his head. "I don't think that's going to work, sir. We're heading home in less than a half hour. We're already at the airport."

Seiffer grunted. "So, catch a different flight. The president wants to see you. Today."

"Hold on, sir." Jake looked at the chair Treavor was sitting in. "Hey, Treavor, the president wants to see us this afternoon."

Treavor sighed. "Aw geez, really?"

"Yep, and I say the heck with him. I don't know about you, but I need some time off to regroup and think about my future."

"I agree. Tell him ... heck, I don't know what to tell him."

"Well, do you want to go?"

"No, I really don't."

"Me either." Jake got back on the phone. "Mr. Seiffer? Tell the president we're not interested."

There was a long pause at the end of the line. "Did you just decline to meet the president of the United States? Are you shitting me?"

"Yes, I did, and Dr. Storm agrees. We need to rethink this arrangement. We both said that we would see how the first mission with the Islamic State went, and I'll tell you, the last part was a freakin' disaster. We lost our close friend, Ted Janick, so tell the man to chill, and we'll reach out when and if we're ready," Jake said forcefully.

Long pause. "He'll be pissed," Seiffer warned.

Jake snorted. "Yeah, he'll get over it. See ya"

As Jake ended the call, Treavor asked. "How did he take it?"

Jake shrugged. "Who gives a shit? Let's go home."

13

BETH ANN MET THEM at the airport and gave Jake a bear hug. Then she drove them to Treavor's house in South Minneapolis and dropped him off.

Treavor opened the front door, strode to the kitchen, and opened the refrigerator. Treavor grinned. Travis had stocked up on Coca-Cola. He popped one open, then headed to his office, where he sat and opened his Bible, looking for a bit of guidance after his harrowing trip.

Treavor flipped to Psalm 16:5-8. "Lord, you're my portion and my cup. You make my lot secure. I keep my eyes always on the Lord. With Him at my right hand, I won't be shaken."

Aha! Now that's understandable. I surely do need God's help. Do I really want to keep doing this government work? How about leading a normal life?. Why the heck not? All right, I'm freakin' invisible, but so what? It's public knowledge, at least in the Twin Cities Maybe I could go back and teach.

Treavor heard the garage door opening and smiled. *Must be Travis.* Treavor strode to the kitchen. The door from the garage opened and Travis came in.

"Hey, Travis."

Travis jumped. "Dang, TS, you scared me."

"Sorry about that."

"That's OK. When did you get back?"

"Early this afternoon. How have you been, little brother?"

Travis tossed his backpack on the floor next to the door. "Fine and dandy, simultaneously," he said with a grin. "Been spending time with my new girlfriend and working a lot."

"Your girl's name is Amber, right?"

"Yeah. She's really nice, and good-looking, too," Travis said proudly.

"Good for you. I'd like to meet her."

"Oh, heck yes. She's dying to see my invisible brother." Then he snorted. "That isn't right."

Treavor chuckled. "I know what you meant, and I'd like to see her as well. Hey, are you hungry? I've been craving corned beef hash, runny eggs, and crispy bacon."

"Hey, I can go for that as long as you're cooking. I'm always hungry."

"I know."

Treavor got busy as Travis sipped a glass of orange juice. "So, TS, tell me about the trip. Did you save the world again?"

"Nope, but Jake and I got rid of some ISIS terrorists. They were going to blow up Westminster Abbey with the queen of England in it."

"Well, I didn't see anything on the news about a church blowing up, so I'm guessing you were successful."

"Yes, we were successful, but the next job wasn't so great."

"Yeah?"

"Yes, we were after more terrorists and it went badly. Ted Janick, a Homeland Security agent, was killed in an explosion. I may have mentioned him to you before."

"That sucks. Hey, Treavor, this stuff you're doing is really dangerous. Are you sure you want to keep it up?"

"That's just what I've been asking myself."

❖❖❖❖❖

Time went on, and Jake and Treavor settled into normal routines. Jake spent most of his time with Beth Ann, who was now a certified veterinarian at a clinic in Eden Prairie. They considered rescheduling their wedding that had been so rudely interrupted by Beth Ann's kidnappers.

Jake started to run in the morning as a result of Treavor's influence. Not at dawn though — that was too damn early for Jake. But the running was good for his lungs and his soul. As he ran, he thought about his future. The death of Ted Janick weighed heavily on his conscience.

But what was really bothering Jake was his power, or curse--this "Just die" ability. *Maybe Treavor is right. "Thou shall not kill." Hey, I have no idea whether or not there is a God, Heaven, or Hell. But if there is a Hell, will I end up there for killing all those people? Hey, they were bad guys, right? The government views me as a hero, but how would God see it? Maybe I should ask Him. Or Her. In any case, I have the power, but I certainly don't need to use it. The president will be pissed off, but who cares? It is my goddamned life, right?*

The next day, the morning air was moist and nippy during his run. As he stopped in front of his home, his cell phone chimed. It was Treavor with an invitation to a dinner next Friday at his parents' place. Beth Ann was also invited.

Jake accepted gratefully. He hung up and pocketed the phone, thinking *It will be good to see Treavor again. Maybe he can help me with my "Just die" dilemma.*

❖❖❖❖❖

Friday arrived, and Jake and Beth Ann took his Jaguar to Treavor's parents' home. It was a modest home in Bloomington, a suburb of Minneapolis, with white siding and green shutters. The grass was well-tended, and there were white and pink hydrangea plants along the front of the home and a large maple tree in the side yard.

Treavor's red Jaguar was parked on the concrete driveway, and Jake slid his yellow Jag up next to it. As Beth Ann hopped out of the passenger seat, the front door opened.

Treavor called out enthusiastically, "Hey, you made it, and you brought your Jag. Cool."

"I did. Hey, how are you, Treavor?"

"I'm good. Hi, Beth Ann, nice to see you." A beautiful woman appeared in the doorway, and Treavor said, "Allow me to introduce you to Eleanor Milburn."

Beth Ann stretched out her hand. "Pleased to meet you."

Eleanor shook her hand. "Likewise."

Treavor said, "Come on in and meet the rest of the crew."

"Sure, lead the way," Jake replied."

As they were introduced, Jake shook Ted Storm's hand and smiled at April. "Wonderful to meet you both. This is my fiancée, Beth Ann."

"Oh, yes, we've heard so much about you. How are you doing? That abduction on your wedding day ... we'll I just can't imagine," April said."

"Yes, it wasn't a fun experience, although I must admit I was treated well," Beth Ann replied.

"Well, I'm glad you're back in one piece."

Beth Ann chuckled. "Me too!"

Ted chimed in. "What would you like to drink? We have water, coffee, Coke and Diet Coke, red and white wine, margaritas, gin-and-tonics, or single malt Scotch, if you like."

Beth Ann smiled. "A margarita sounds wonderful."

"Follow me. You can meet Travis and his girlfriend. Jake, do you want anything?"

Jake shook his head. "I'm good for now ... maybe a little wine with dinner."

"OK, you bet," said Ted. He and Beth Ann turned and headed to the kitchen with April right on their heels.

Treavor turned to Jake and Eleanor. "Come on, Tanya and Easton are in the living room."

Treavor's sister Tanya was seated on the couch next to her fiancé Easton Carter. Carter rose and extended a hand to Jake, flashing a welcoming smile. "Good to see you again, Jake. It's been too long."

"Hey, Easton, you're looking spiffy," Jake said.

Tanya stood up. "Hi, Jake. Introduce me to this beautiful young woman. I assume this is Beth Ann?"

"I am, indeed. Nice to meet you," responded Beth Ann.

Tanya motioned to the couch. "Please, sit next to me."

Ted arrived with Beth Ann's margarita and handed it to her with a slight bow. "I topped it off with a splash of Grand Marnier. I hope you like it that way."

Beth Ann took the wide-rimmed glass, careful not to spill any. "That's perfect, thank you."

"My pleasure," Ted said. He glanced at Tanya. "Would you like one?"

Tanya grinned. "I would love one, but I'm pregnant."

Ted gasped. "Oh my gosh, that's wonderful." Then he yelled over his shoulder, "April, Tanya's pregnant!"

Tanya rolled her eyes and laughed as April came bustling into the living room holding a tall glass of gin and tonic. "Really, Tanya? You're pregnant?"

"Uh-huh. I took a home pregnancy test a week ago, then went to my doctor to confirm. I'm four weeks' pregnant."

"Hooray!" April exclaimed and clapped her hands. "Grandchildren at last!" She paused as her brows knitted together. "When is the wedding?" she asked warily.

Tanya shook her head. "We don't know yet. Heck, this was unexpected."

Easton grunted. "I'll say."

❖❖❖❖❖

Ted and April served a dinner fit for Thanksgiving or Christmas—honey baked ham, scalloped potatoes, macaroni and cheese, green bean casserole, sweet potato soufflé, and pumpkin pie.

Amber sat across the table from Treavor. She was mesmerized as she watched things appearing and disappearing from the table as Treavor picked them up and laid them down. She leaned closer to Travis and whispered, "Would you introduce me to Treavor?"

Travis pushed his lower lip out. "Sure, of course. Hey, TS, I'd like you to meet my friend Amber Slone."

"Hello, Amber. I've heard wonderful things about you," Treavor said pleasantly.

Amber blushed and elbowed Travis. "Thank you, but your brother may have been exaggerating," she said modestly.

Across the table, Eleanor was asking Tanya about her early life. "I understand you were in the army for a number of years. What made you enlist?"

Tanya pursed her lips. "Actually, it's an interesting story. I was kind of a rebellious teenager and had gotten involved with the wrong group of friends. One night, I was in a car with someone when he did a drive-by shooting. The man didn't die, and he identified us, so all four of us were arrested. The judge gave me two choices—I could go to Stillwater Prison for five years or enlist in the army. I had just turned eighteen, and I chose the army, of course." She stopped and frowned. "That's when female recruits were rare and considered sport."

Eleanor shook her head slightly. "What do you mean?"

Tanya snorted. "What I mean is that three rednecks tried to rape me in the women's shower."

Eleanor brought a hand to her mouth. "My God, Tanya, that's terrible!"

Tanya chuckled quietly. "Not really. The maintenance crew had been doing some plumbing repairs in there, so I grabbed a loose three-foot pipe and damn near beat them to death with it." She laughed again. "If my sister soldiers hadn't intervened, I would've killed them all. No one messed with me after that, man or woman."

"Anyway, I stayed in for twenty years and mustered out as one of the first female majors," she said proudly. "Took my pension and was a cop in Minneapolis for a few years. I had done a number of assignments with the Bureau of Criminal Apprehension. They offered me a position, and here I am."

Eleanor took a sip of her drink. "Oh, so you're in law enforcement. Is that how you met Easton?"

"Uh-huh. We had a long string of bank robberies here in the Twin Cities and Easton, Treavor, and I teamed up on that. From there ... I guess nature just took its course."

Eleanor giggled and whispered, "I'll say. My gosh, he's a handsome man."

Tanya flashed a quick smile. "Yes, he is, and a good man. Strong values, loyal to a fault, and he loves me unequivocally."

Eleanor reached over and patted her on the hand. "You can tell." Then she leaned in close and muttered, "Don't tell a soul, but I missed my last period, and it looks like I'm getting morning sickness."

"Oh my God! Are you pregnant too?" whispered Tanya.

Eleanor smiled shyly and shrugged. "Yeah, I think so."

❖ ❖ ❖ ❖ ❖

At the end of the meal, Treavor talked about his and Jake's latest adventures in London—thwarting the bombing at Westminster Abbey with Queen Elizabeth II in attendance, then the disaster at the apartment building and the death of Ted Janick.

His father asked, "Have you gotten a new assignment yet?"

Treavor waited a moment before he replied. "Actually, the president asked Jake and I to come to the White House, but we declined."

Ted Storm shook his head vigorously. "You were summoned to the White House and didn't go? That's crazy. It's un-American."

Jake peered across the table and considered Ted. "I respectfully beg to disagree. I must tell you, I'm tired of this killing, but I knew I would've agreed to do whatever he wanted if I came in. He's a very persuasive person."

"Well, goddammit, you should've gone and done what he asked you to do. This is for the good of the country. We're at war with the Islamic State, and you have a unique power. I flew jets for the navy and killed a lot of people—some innocent civilians—and I'll tell you, I never lost a wink of sleep over it. That's war, plain and simple. I say do your duty!"

"Really? How about your invisible son? He won't kill people. Says it's against God's will."

"That's right," confirmed Treavor.

Ted shook his head. "That's baloney, Treavor. You killed the two hijackers on the Delta flight, as I recall."

Treavor sucked in a breath. "I didn't have time to think about it. In hindsight, maybe I could've just subdued them."

Ted snorted. "That's bullshit, son. Do your fucking duty, for Christ's sake." He got up from the table and stalked off.

Treavor shook his invisible head. "Well, I guess we know where he stands," he said.

14

IT WAS TWO WEEKS LATER when Treavor received a call from Tony Seiffer. "Dr. Storm, sir, how are you?"

Treavor scoffed. "Sir? Really? That's a first, you calling me sir, but I'm fine. And how are you ... sir?"

"As well as can be expected, but I must tell you, POTUS wasn't pleased that you and Mr. Silver blew him off before you left D.C."

"Yeah, I guess people don't tell him 'no' very often. Well, he'll cool off."

"Yes, he already has. But now he needs both of you for an immediate mission ... and he said to say 'please'."

"Wow. This sounds ominous."

"Yeah, it is. There's a big gathering of Islamic State leaders in the Spīn Ghar Mountain Range, otherwise known as the White Mountains, on the border with Pakistan and Afghanistan."

"Okay. And?"

"Um ... the president would be eternally grateful if you and Jake crashed the party. This meeting is a rare opportunity, and you'd be doing your country a great service. The entire free world, actually."

"Yeah, if it goes well. That last job in London sure didn't."

"Yes, we all know that, and the loss of Ted Janick was a tragedy. But life goes on, and so does evil. We really need you, Dr. Storm."

Treavor sighed. "Listen, I'm good with it, so count me in. But Jake ... well, I can't speak for him. Ted's death really shook him up. I really don't think he'll agree to it."

"Yes, that's what we've heard through the grapevine, but we have an alternate plan if you're willing to participate."

"What's that?"

"We have a young Marine who's a hell of a shot with any type of firearm. He'll take Jake's place if Mr. Silver declines."

"Hmm ... how big is he? If he weighs too much, I wouldn't be able to carry him."

"He's short and slim, which is one of the reasons we selected him."

"And when is this big meeting?"

"Three days from today, so we will need you to come in right away."

"OK, sign me up, but understand, Jake is iffy. Have you called him?"

"Yes, I have, and he isn't returning my calls. Perhaps you could persuade him?"

"Hey, I won't pressure him, but I'll tell him about the assignment and see what he says."

"All right, please let me know soon. Your plane leaves for Washington tomorrow morning."

"Gotcha. I'll let you know after I've talked to Jake."

"Thank you, sir. The president will be very pleased."

"Sure, that's great. Goodbye."

Treavor looked at the cell phone and shook his head. "What did I just do?" he murmured.

❖❖❖❖❖

Treavor dialed Jake and got his answering machine. Jake's message was brief and to the point. "Sorry, I'm not available. You know what to do."

"Hey, Jake, it's Treavor. Give me a call, please."

Treavor went to the fridge, grabbed a Coke, and sipped it, wondering whether he'd ever see his home again. He was under no delusions. *These missions are dangerous. Invisibility is no guarantee that I won't be killed, especially if I don't have Jake along.*

Just then, the phone rang. "Hey, Jake, how's it going?" Treavor asked tentatively.

"I'm fine, Treavor. How about you?"

"Pretty good. Um, Jake, I got a call from Tony Seiffer, and POTUS would like us to go on another mission."

Jake sighed. "Yeah, I saw that he had called me as well, but I didn't return the call. I'm still having second thoughts about all the killing. I mean, it's for a good cause, but ..."

"I know, it weighs you down. Hey, man, I don't blame you. You know how I feel about taking a human life."

"Yes, I do. In fact, I just might be coming around to your way of thinking."

"So, do you want me to say you aren't interested?"

The line was silent for a while. "You still there, Jake?" Treavor asked.

"Tell me about the mission."

"There's going to be a big meeting of most of the Islamic State leaders in the Afghan mountains. The plan is to take them all out."

"Are you going to do it?"

Treavor paused. "Yes, I said I would."

"Even if I don't come along?"

"Yes. They have a young soldier who will take your place. He's supposed to be very proficient with firearms."

"From what you told me, he sure better be."

"Yes, that's right. He'll have my life in his hands."

There was another long silence. "I'm assuming that you aren't coming?" Treavor asked.

"I can't, Treavor. I just can't."

"I get it, my friend."

"Listen, Treavor, go with God, and I'll be praying for you."

Treavor laughed quietly. "You pray, Jake? That's a first."

Jake grunted. "Hey, I'm turning over a new leaf. I might even start reading the Bible."

Then they both laughed, with a tinge of sadness.

❖❖❖❖❖

Treavor was picked up early the next morning. The driver, a young Marine, was aware that his fare was invisible, and he shrugged it off. He drove to the airport and the separate field for the National Guard planes, around back and up to a chain-link fence, which a guard opened. They then proceeded to a separate part of the tarmac where a gleaming blue and white Grumman C20-B sat idling.

Treavor was met at the bottom of the steps by the chief assistant to the president's chief of staff. He gave just a bit of a start when Treavor set his duffel bag on the tarmac in front of him. He flashed a gaunt smile. "I assume you're Dr. Storm, standing next to that duffel?"

"Yes, sir, I am."

"Well, nice to meet you, sir. My name is Richard Young. Please follow me."

After a comfortable flight in the specially equipped government twelve-seater, they landed at Andrews Air Force Base. In the D.C. sky, dark clouds were churning on the horizon, and the sky was turning an ominous gray. Treavor followed Richard to a waiting SUV. They climbed into the roomy back seat as a few raindrops began to fall.

Thirty minutes later, Treavor followed Richard through the security checkpoint as he wound through halls, finally reaching the Oval Office waiting room. The elderly receptionist pushed a button on her desk phone and picked up the handset. "Mr. Young is here to see you, sir," she stated. She hung up the phone. "The president will see you now," she said with a quick nod.

Richard moved toward the door, and Seiffer opened it. "Come in, Richard. I assume you have Dr. Storm with you?"

"Yes, sir," Richard replied.

"I'm here," Treavor said unenthusiastically.

"Good of you to come, Dr. Storm. Please come in."

The president nodded to Richard Young; and smiled. "Dr. Storm, it sounds like you're not enthused to be here."

"Well, sir, I'm here and Jake Silver isn't."

POTUS drew in a sharp breath. "Yes, I know, and thank you, sir, for volunteering for this mission." He turned and looked at a uniformed Marine. "Let me introduce you to Lieutenant Garcia." The marine rose crisply as the president introduced him. He stood absolutely erect, getting the most out of his five-foot-two height. His eyes were sharp and quick, and he exuded a vibe of "don't fucking mess with me." Treavor knew right then and there that the small Marine could back it up.

"Hello, lieutenant. My name is Treavor Storm, and I guess we will be working together."

"Yes, sir," Garcia responded.

Treavor laughed to himself. "Put your hand out, lieutenant, and I'll give it a shake."

The lieutenant turned to the president, who nodded, then stuck his hand out toward Treavor's voice, and Treavor shook the soldier's hand. His grip was firm and relentless, and his lip twisted up into a brief smile as he squeezed.

Treavor smothered a chuckle. He was drawn to the man and decided then and there that he'd continue with the mission. "I'm glad to be working with you, Lt. Garcia."

The president spoke up. "Dr. Storm, do you play golf?"

"Yes, sir. Well, I did before I became invisible."

"Ah, yes. Well, after this is done, I'd like you to play a round with me."

Treavor smiled halfheartedly. "That would be fine, sir."

POTUS sucked in a breath. "Okay, down to business. As we discussed, the leaders of the Islamic State are gathering on a mountain that borders Pakistan and Afghanistan. They lost a lot of people after your last outing with Jake, and their replacements will be attending the meeting as well as the top leaders. It's an opportunity we just can't pass up. Garcia is familiar with the terrain. Right, lieutenant?"

"Yes, sir. Absolutely."

"Very good. Tony, tell them the rest, will you?"

"Yes, sir," Seiffer replied. "It's a simple plan. Dr Storm, Lt. Garcia, and a squad of Marines will land in a Black Hawk helicopter two or so klicks from the caves. You will all hike to the caves and terminate everyone inside. Then you will get the hell out of there in one piece."

"Wow. That's it?" Treavor asked. "That doesn't sound like much of a plan."

"Dr. Storm, these men are specialists in this type of operation. You will be there with the best, and with your special ability, it should all go like clockwork."

"I sure hope you're right. When do we leave?"

"Tomorrow, so get some rest tonight and eat well."

Treavor's stomach rumbled loudly, and everyone grinned. "Speaking of eating, I'm starved. There wasn't much to eat on the flight over."

The president frowned. "Well, we're all done here. Tony, take Dr. Storm down to the mess hall and get him something to eat, for Christ's sake."

The president stood held out his hand, which Treavor clasped and shook. "Go with God, Dr. Storm, and come back in one piece. I would really like to have that round of golf. I've never golfed with an invisible man before. I'm sure it will be very interesting."

Everyone trooped down to the White House Mess, which was in the basement of the West Wing. The US Navy operates it, and it can accommodate about fifty diners. It was lined with light-brown paneling, and numerous paintings of old-time sailing vessels adorned the walls. The chief of staff sat next to Treavor and ordered for him—a double cheeseburger, onion rings, and a Coca-Cola.

The chief leaned close to Treavor and motioned toward the lieutenant. "Lt. Garcia graduated at the top of his class at the Marine Corps University. He was born here in the States. His parents are migrant farm workers who return to Mexico after the crops are brought in. Other than Jake Silver, you couldn't have a better partner. The man won't back down. He has received the Silver Star and a Purple Heart. And don't let his size fool you. He carried one of his wounded men ten miles on his shoulders. Saved the man's life."

"He seems very competent. Doesn't talk much, though," replied Treavor.

"Oh, he will when he has something to say."

"So, who's in charge, the lieutenant or me?"

"That would be the lieutenant."

"Really? I'm not sure that I agree with that."

The chief laughed. "Hey, you're the invisible dude. If it comes down to it, I'm guessing you can do whatever the hell you want!"

Treavor grunted. "That's right."

15

Jake Silver finished his breakfast and jumped on his twenty-speed Cannondale bicycle. He headed down the path behind his home toward Lake Calhoun, where his friend Leslie Scarmuzzo would soon be performing a Fourth of July concert with her band Retro Groove.

Jake pumped the bike around the lakes, slowing down for pedestrians and assorted dogs. Then his cell phone chimed and he pulled it out of his jacket pocket. It was Beth Ann. He coasted off the bike path and stopped.

"Hey, Beth Ann, how's it going?"

"I'm good, sweetheart. I'm on my lunch break, so I can't talk long. I just wondered whether you made up your mind about the mission with Treavor."

"I don't know yet. I'm at Lake Calhoun, biking and trying to decide."

"Oh, nice. Good day for a ride, and I know how a ride clears your mind."

"Well, not so far. I'm still torn."

"Well, I know you'll figure it out." She paused. "I love you either way."

Jake smiled at that. "Thanks, sweet pea, I know you do. I love you, too."

"I have to go. Call me or text me once you decide, okay?"

"Sure, will do. Bye."

Jake gazed at the lake, sparkling with the sun shining on the small ripples. A group of five compact sailboats was moving along with the warm breeze. Quite a few fishing boats were also on the lake, the fishermen casting their lures toward the shore, hoping to catch a tiger muskie. All in all, it was a glorious, sunny day, and the blue sky was dotted with white clouds that looked like large cotton balls.

Jake headed back to his home in Victoria, more than thirty miles away--plenty of time to think. By the time he wheeled his bike into his garage, he had made his decision.

He put his bike away, headed to the bathroom, and jumped in the shower. Afterward, he dressed in blue jeans and a black shirt with a Beatles' Abbey Road imprint on it, a gift from Travis.

Jake called the White House and asked to speak to Tony Seiffer. He was unavailable, so Jake left a voicemail. "This is Jake Silver. Please call me as soon as you get this."

A half hour later, Jake's cell phone chirped.

"Mr. Silver?"

"Yes, that's me."

"Please hold for the president of the United States."

A minute later, a familiar voice came over the phone. "Mr. Silver, this is the president. I'm returning your call to Tony Seiffer, as he's a bit tied up with your invisible friend."

"Thank you," Jake replied. "How are you doing, sir?"

The president snorted. "I'd feel a lot better if you were here with the good doctor."

"Well, sir, that's why I called. I have reconsidered, and I'd like to join the mission if it's not too late."

"By God, that's fantastic! And no, it's not too late, but boy, we're cutting it close." The president paused as he talked to someone in the room. "Someone will call you back within minutes. In the meantime, pack a bag for the mountains of Afghanistan. We will arrange a flight out for you And thank you, Jake. You're the ultimate patriot."

Twenty minutes later, Jake had just finished packing when his cell chirped.

"Is this Mr. Jake Silver?" a new voice asked.

"Yes, it is."

"This is Richard Young, assistant to Mr. Seiffer. Please get a ride to Best Jets International at 711 Eaton Street in St. Paul as quickly as possible. You will be met there and taken to your plane."

"Okay. Is there anything else I need to do?"

"No, sir, just get moving, and thank you. It's good to have you aboard."

Jake sighed and said nothing.

❖❖❖❖❖

Jake jumped in his Mercedes and wasted no time getting to the St. Paul airstrip. It wasn't rush hour, so the trip took less than forty minutes. On the way, he phoned Beth Ann and got her voicemail.

"Darling, I'm going. Sorry I couldn't say goodbye in person, but things are moving fast and I'm already on my way out of the country. Whatever happens, I love you and will do everything I can to be back soon."

He pulled up to the main building and hurried inside. The fellow behind the counter asked, "Can I help you?"

"Yes you can. I'm Jake Silver."

"Ah, yes, Mr. Silver. I've been expecting you. Your pilot is already on board. Please follow me." As they moved through the terminal, the man said, "It's not every day that we get a call from the president's chief of staff." He opened a door, and they headed toward a jet that was waiting on the tarmac.

"This Dassault Falcon 900DX had been reserved for the CEO of 3M," he said as they approached the jet. "But he understood that it was being commandeered by the government for use in a national emergency. So, whoever you are, Mr. Silver, good luck and God bless."

"Thanks," Jake said quietly and headed up the stairs with his duffel bag.

Yeah, I'm going to need good luck. Maybe God will bless the mission, too.

❖ ❖ ❖ ❖ ❖

Treavor was in his hotel suite, paging through the Gideon's Bible and reading Psalm 23:4. "Even though I walk through the darkest valley, I will fear no evil for You are with me: Your rod and Your staff, they comfort me."

Treavor grunted silently as he finished. *I hope so. Maybe Lt. Garcia and his skill with weapons could replace the Lord's rod and staff.*

He closed the Bible and was beginning to put it back in the end table when someone knocked on his door. Treavor peered through the peephole and smiled broadly. He quickly opened the door. "Jake, what are you doing here?"

Jake grunted and smiled as well. "Well, I changed my mind, and here I am. I couldn't let you get all the glory."

Treavor cried out with joy. "Yeah, right. Boy, am I glad to see you. Come on in."

Once in the room, Jake saw the Bible on the bed and picked it up. "Do you read this often?"

Treavor nodded. "Nearly every day. It gives me wisdom and comfort."

"I could sure use some of that. Maybe I should take it up."

"It couldn't hurt. So, what changed your mind about coming along on this mission?"

"Well, I'd been thinking about what your father said at dinner about doing your duty. And he was right. Also, I didn't want to leave you hanging. This could be the most dangerous mission so far. So I went for a long bike ride to clear my head, and by the time I was done, I knew what I had to do."

"You're right about how dangerous this is going to be." Treavor said, then smiled widely. "But now that you're here, I sure feel better about our ability to pull it off."

Jake said nothing. He just bobbed his head while clinging to the Bible.

❖❖❖❖❖

On the long flight to Afghanistan, Lt. Garcia sat down next to Jake with a dubious expression. "Sir, am I to understand that you can point at people, say 'Just die,' and they do?"

Jake nodded. "Yes, lieutenant, that's correct. It works on animals as well."

Garcia sat and thought about that for a bit. "Well, sir, this is the most interesting mission I've ever been on. First an invisible man, and now you."

Jake flashed a half grin. "I imagine so."

"That's amazing. I think I'd like to have this power, sir."

Jake shook his head. "Be careful what you wish for, lieutenant. It's a blessing, but mostly a curse."

Garcia looked into Jake's eyes, then nodded slightly. "Yes, I can see how it could be a terrible burden," he said quietly.

"You have no idea," Jake replied sadly.

❖❖❖❖❖

The jet landed at Islamabad International Airport, and the Pakistani Army had the Black Hawk ready to go. Several of the helicopters had been given to Pakistan a couple of years ago, and they were more than willing to allow them to be used for the mission.

The US crew was led past a group of buildings. There were large hangars for jets and helicopters, an administrative building, sleeping quarters, and finally, a mess hall, which they utilized with gusto. They then retired to their quarters to try to get a bit of sleep before leaving.

That evening the crew gathered, boarded the helicopter, and flew off. They stopped once at the Pakistan-Afghanistan border to refuel before departing for the White Mountains. During the flight in the noisy copter, Treavor and Jake silently wondered if this would be their final mission.

It was late afternoon when the Black Hawk landed at its designated spot, nearly halfway up the mountain. As the rotors quit spinning, Treavor studied Jake as he unbuckled his seat belt.

"Jake, are you ready for this, or do you want to stay here?"

"Nope, I'm good. Let's get this thing over with," Jake replied. He stood and climbed out of the helicopter, then moved toward Lt. Garcia, who was giving last-minute instructions to his men.

"Remember, do not engage the enemy unless fired upon," Garcia concluded. The Marines had small lights on their helmets and GPS watches on their wrists. Garcia turned to Jake and the invisible Treavor. "Are you both ready?"

Jake nodded and Treavor replied, "As ready as we'll ever be, lieutenant. Please lead the way."

They proceeded in staggered file, M4A1s in their hands with a grenade launcher attached under the barrel. Garcia led the way with a man behind him, Treavor next, Jake fourth. The three remaining Marines brought up the rear, their heads on a swivel.

They took it slowly at first and made their way up the mountain, weaving through the rocks and boulders. It was eerily quiet. The butterball moon passed in and out of the ragged figures of the dark clouds, and the stars sparkled above in the velvety heavens like glistening diamonds. There was no wind at all, and the temperature was moderate. After about two kilometers, Lt. Garcia glanced at his wrist, then squatted down and turned to Jake. "We will wait here until dawn."

❖ ❖ ❖ ❖ ❖

Back in Minnesota, Eleanor, Beth Ann, and Tanya were meeting for a very early breakfast at the Original Pancake House. Beth Ann had organized the meeting. She had good news and wanted to share it.

Eleanor was showing her pregnancy, but Tanya was not quite there yet. The three women were silent as they nursed their coffees and perused the extensive menu. A few minutes later, the waitress came over to take their orders. Eleanor chose Eggs Benedict with a side of hash browns; Tanya selected cinnamon-apple pancakes topped with caramelized apples, two soft-boiled eggs over easy, and a side of bacon;

and Beth Ann decided on the corned beef hash with two eggs, sunny-side up, and blueberry pancakes. They all opted for the freshly squeezed orange juice.

Tanya glanced across the booth's table. "So, Beth Ann, this was a great idea. We should do it more often." Eleanor nodded as she sipped her hot, aromatic coffee.

Beth Ann smiled gently. "Yes, that would be wonderful, but just to let you know, this meal is on me."

Tanya pursed her lips. "Now, you don't have to do that."

Beth Ann shook her head. "No, I insist. This is a celebration."

"Really? A celebration of what?" Eleanor asked.

Beth Ann grinned from ear to ear "Well, you two are pregnant, and I was feeling left out, so ..."

"Are you kidding me!" exclaimed Tanya.

Beth Ann bobbed her head. "Yep, three weeks pregnant. The doctor confirmed it just yesterday."

"Oh my God!" Eleanor proclaimed. "That's incredible. That's just ... just wonderful!"

Beth Ann's eyes gleamed. "Yes, it is, isn't it?"

"Does Jake know?" asked Tanya.

"No, he doesn't. At the moment, he's out of town on another mission for the president."

"Really? I thought he was giving that up."

"Well, apparently, he changed his mind."

"I assume he's with Treavor and headed for Afghanistan?" Eleanor inquired.

"Yes, indeed." Then Beth Ann paused. "I only hope they both come home in one piece. I don't want to be a single parent."

Eleanor drew in a quick breath. "Amen to that."

❖❖❖❖❖

Dawn came gradually on the White Mountain range, and with it purple and gray clouds on the distant horizon. The crew moved silently to a ridge overlooking the caves. Outside the entrances was a crude training course about fifty yards long. A few of the Marines whispered to each other, as they recognized the setup as a makeshift imitation of their own basic training ground. Lt. Garcia had his men spread out, with Jake and Treavor at his side.

As the sun rose, a tall, bearded man came out of a cave with a two-foot mat, knelt, and began to pray. More men then exited the caves, set their own prayer mats down, and the murmur of prayers mingled with a cough or two to break the morning's silence.

Treavor turned to Garcia. "What's the plan?"

"There are many more in the caves. We should wait until they all come out."

"Well, what if they don't?"

The lieutenant grunted. "Well, that's why we brought you along. We could kill all of them without you, but who knows how long those caves are and whether or not there's another exit. You both will need to go in and have Mr. Silver do his 'Just die' thing."

"Why don't I just do it now, with these guys?" asked Jake.

The lieutenant shook his head. "Just wait. There's no need to hurry."

The men soon finished their prayers, then rose and went back into their respective caves. After a bit, the smell of cooking wafted out of each of the caves. Treavor's stomach rumbled, and Jake chuckled quietly. "Are you hungry again, Treavor?" Treavor grunted but said nothing.

The sun rose in the intensely blue sky. The purple clouds of dawn were now white, fluffy, and nearly stationary, and the crew waited for close to an hour. Finally, men began emerging from the caves. Some were holding new AK-12 assault rifles, others had older model AK-75 models, and a few had Soviet-era AK-47s. A small group was unarmed, most likely the senior leaders.

As the last men exited the caves, Lt. Garcia turned, eyeballed Jake, and nodded. "Do your thing, Mr. Silver."

Jake, who was lying down and facing the men, wiggled his fingers on his right hand and yelled "Just die" over and over again. The terrorists began to drop like flies. A few in the back raised their rifles and got off a shot in the direction of Jake's voice, but Jake pointed at each of them and they collapsed like bags of garbage until every one of them was dead.

Lt. Garcia and his Marines were stunned. They had never seen anything like it. "Holy shit!" one Marine exclaimed. Another answered, "Holy shit is right." Lt. Garcia turned back to Jake. "I wouldn't have believed it if I didn't see it with my own two eyes."

Just then, automatic rifles poked out of the three occupied caves, and fire began spraying Jake's location with bullets. Lt. Garcia bellowed out, "Return fire."

The Marines spewed fire and death from their M4A1s. Their bullets were followed by grenades launched into one cave after another ... whump after whump ... until the rifle shots from the caves ceased. But still the Marines poured it on, caught up in the moment. Finally, Lt. Garcia shouted out, "Cease fire," as smoke billowed out of the half-dozen caves.

It was now as silent as the inside of a coffin. There was no wind, no breeze. Nothing. The dark, black-and-gray smoke from the grenades hung in the air with nowhere to go. The scene in front of the caves was macabre, with numerous terrorists' bodies covered with smoke, ash, and rock fragments. The sky turned suddenly cloudy, perhaps a tribute to the massacre. Turkey vultures were soaring overhead, waiting for the tasty human morsels.

Jake spoke to Treavor. "Do you think it's over?"

"Heck, I don't know, partner. I'm just along for the ride. I guess you guys didn't really need me."

Lt. Garcia approached them, having overheard their conversation. "Sorry, guys, but we're not done yet."

Jake frowned. "You don't think anyone could have survived that, do you?"

The lieutenant shrugged. "I have no idea, but that's where your skills come into play."

"So, what do you want us to do?" Treavor inquired.

"Clear each cave out. Go to the back and see whether there are any survivors, then do what you do best," Garcia said, eyeing Jake.

Jake nodded slightly. "Well, we came all this way, so we might as well finish the job."

"Exactly. My Marines will provide cover until you get inside. You never know who might have heard the shots."

Treavor eyed Jake. "How do you want to do it this time ... fireman's carry or you on my back?" he asked.

"On your back, buddy."

"OK, give me your hand."

Treavor took Jake's hand, placed it on his shoulder, then turned. Jake grabbed one shoulder, then the other.

"My hands are behind me," said Treavor. "Jump up when you're ready."

Jake paused, then jumped. Treavor grasped Jake behind the knees, and after adjusting himself, Jake settled in and disappeared.

Garcia gave a yelp. "Wow, that's amazing. You men are something else!"

Jake laughed softly. "Yes, we are."

With Jake on his back, Treavor marched to the lip of the cave, then paused and listened intently. There was no sound, and he whispered to Jake, "Let's check it out."

The cave wasn't deep, perhaps thirty-five feet, and it was decimated. The grenades had done their work. Body parts were strewn everywhere, and blood coated the walls.

"Jesus Christ," Jake murmured.

Treavor nodded his head. "Amen to that. Let's get out of here. There's nothing more to do in this one."

The next cave was wider and a bit deeper than the first. The grenades had again proved deadly, as well as the assault rifles. There were three men in the back of the cave pushed up against the cave wall, all riddled with bullets. One terrorist was completely missing the top of his head, with only his nose and below intact. A long beard hung to the middle of his chest. It had been gray, but now was covered in crimson, the red essence of life dripping into his lap.

There were two other men near the first man, both younger by the look of their dark beards. One man's lower legs were pummeled with bullets and blood. The other had taken slugs to his chest and abdomen, and his intestines were partially exposed.

"Son of a bitch," Jake murmured.

Treavor didn't respond. He just turned and left, still carrying the invisible Jake on his back.

There was only one cave left, and Treavor and Jake cautiously entered it. The entrance was larger than the other caves, letting in more daylight. The front part of the cave was a morbid mess, just like the other two. Even more so. There was blood everywhere, body parts strewn all over. Even a decapitated head. The cave was different from the others in that it stretched back much farther than the other two. Then the two men heard a distant cough.

Jake whispered to Treavor, "Sounds like someone here is still alive."

"Yeah, it sure does."

As they deliberately approached the back of the cave, the light diminished until they saw only shadows. Treavor carefully moved along, avoiding rocks and small boulders. The smoke from the grenades was still thick when he stopped. There was a small kerosene lantern on the floor about ten feet in front of him. A man stood on one side of it, apparently uninjured, with an assault rifle held in front of his chest.

A thick plume of smoke entered Jake's lungs and he coughed. The man raised his rifle and fired. Jake yelped and grabbed his left bicep. "Goddammit, I'm shot." Then he fell off Treavor's back, now visible. The terrorist jerked his head back at the sight of Jake appearing out of thin air right in front of him, then started to raise his rifle. Treavor lunged forward and slammed into the man, pushing him back and over with a tackle that would have made his high school football coach proud. The man's rifle flew into the air and bounced off the back wall of the cave. The terrorist had no idea what he had been hit with, but he was still very much a danger, rolling over and crawling toward his weapon. Treavor glanced at Jake, who was in no shape to help. He was holding his bicep with his right hand and groaning.

The terrorist gripped his assault rifle and swung it toward the injured Jake Silver with a wicked grin on his weathered face. He began to squeeze the trigger just as Treavor grabbed the barrel of the gun and pushed it toward the ceiling. Bullets hit the rock cave roof and ricocheted in all directions. Treavor ripped the assault rifle away from the man, flipped it up, and clubbed him under the chin with the stock. The man fell backward, smacking his head on the cave wall with a loud thunk. His eyes rolled up and blood poured from the back of his head. He shuddered and gasped, then slid down the rock wall, dead before he came to rest on the cave floor.

Treavor froze. Once again, he had killed another human being. He stood in place for a moment or two, then Jake groaned. Treavor sighed with remorse, then turned and moved quickly to Jake. His shirt sleeve was drenched with blood, and it was obvious that he was in pain. Treavor stripped off his shirt, moved Jake's hand off the bicep wound, then wrapped it tightly with a sleeve of his shirt.

Then he heard a voice behind him, and he turned. There stood a rail-thin man, with a long, salt-and-pepper beard and long hair the same color, clutching the dead man's assault rifle and pointing it at Jake. He squeezed the trigger and ... nothing happened. The long gun was out of bullets. The man's eyebrows knitted together, and he frowned as he tossed the rifle aside.

Then he spoke in perfect English, "I've heard rumors that my American adversaries had an invisible man in their ranks, but I didn't believe it until now."

Treavor studied the man. He looked very familiar, then it dawned on him. This was Ayoub Umar Habib, the leader of the Islamic State.

"Yes, my name is Dr. Treavor Storm, and I am, indeed, invisible." He paused. "And you're Habib."

"You're correct," Habib said. Then he laughed softly. "It's a pleasure to meet you, Dr. Storm."

"I can't say the same."

Habib shrugged, then his gaze shifted behind Jake and Treavor. Lt. Garcia spoke from behind them. "Dr. Storm, what happened to Mr. Silver?"

"He was shot. Looks like it's a through and through in his left bicep."

The lieutenant turned his head, the light of his helmet shining brightly on Jake. "Alberto and Marcos, take Mr. Silver out of here."

The two Marines help Jake up and out of the cave as Lt. Garcia kept Habib covered with his rifle. He gestured to the terrorist. "Hands in the air," he commanded.

Habib shook his head. "No, go ahead and shoot me."

Garcia raised his M4A1 and began to squeeze the trigger when Treavor spoke up. "Lieutenant, stop, don't do it. There has been enough killing for one day."

Lt. Garcia hesitated, then Jake called out softly. "Treavor is right, lieutenant. Enough is enough."

Garcia sighed and lowered his weapon. "All right." Then he flashed a cutting grin. "I'm sure the black site boys will be happy to see him." He turned to the last of his Marines. "Zip tie this asshole, and let's bug out to the Black Hawk. Who knows who heard those shots."

They hiked down the mountain quickly, carrying Jake and pushing Habib ahead of them. Fortunately, the two-kilometer hike was uneventful, as was the flight back to Pakistan. Jake was tended to first in the helicopter, then in Pakistan in the army's hospital. His wound was, indeed, a through and through. Some meat lost, but no bone or artery.

Jake and Treavor climbed into a Homeland Security jet and winged their way home, happy to be alive.

❖❖❖❖❖

Two months later, in Pastor Thomas Storm's church, Treavor married Eleanor, Tanya married Easton, and Jake finally married Beth Ann. Easton and Tanya were driven to the reception in a limousine, Jake and Beth Ann drove in their canary yellow 1970XKE, and Treavor and Eleanor drove in his convertible, fire-engine red 1971XKE, with Treavor at the wheel. All three brides were varying degrees of pregnant. Jake and Beth Ann were expecting a boy, who was to be named Ted, after Ted Janick.

The capture of Habib led to the identification, location, and slaying of the few leaders who weren't at the meeting on the White Mountain range. Finally, the Islamic State was no more, and the world could breathe easier.

Amen.

Acknowledgements

I would like to acknowledge my writing team.

Ken Schubert, my jack-of-all-trades, publisher, and Amazon go-between.

Joyce Mochrie, owner of One Last Look, my copy editor who has no peer.

My talented graphic artist, Elana Karoumpali, who is available through 99designs.

All of the folks at Chanticleer International for manuscript review and the follow-up, including the lovely Kiffer Brown.

Also, my writing backstop, Melinda Nelson of Excelsior. I don't know what I would do without her.

And finally, you the reader, for it would all be for naught without your participation.

Peace,

E. Alan Fleischauer

About the Author

E. Alan Fleischauer is an award-winning poet and a multi-award-winning author.

This paranormal thriller, *The Doctor Is Invisible,* is his thirteenth book and continues the characters and themes of his previous novels *Just Die* and *The Doctor is Invisible.*.

Just Die won first place in the Chanticleer International Paranormal Category. It is about a financial planner who has a mild stroke, only to wake up and realize that he can point at animals and people, say "Just die," and they do just that. It introduces Jake Silver and his fight to deal with this special power—or curse. *Just Die* is an Amazon best seller.

The Doctor is Invisible introduces Dr. Treavor Storm, a young professor whose life is turned upside-down by a freak accident that renders him invisible. As he struggles to adjust, his condition attracts the attention of people who would use it for good or evil ends.

His new non-fiction book *Reconfigurement* is getting rave reviews. It is focused on planning ahead, working at a job that you love, and having lots of fun before you retire.

Mr. Fleischauer's Western series introduced JT Thomas as his protagonist. The first book, *Rescued*, was awarded the Laramie Award First Prize as the Best Americana Western of 2019. Mr. Fleischauer's follow-up novel in the series is *Hunted* (a finalist for the Laramie Award). *Kidnapped* has also been published, as well as *Tommies*, the fourth book, and then *JT's World*, the last book in the series. The series won first prize in the Western Series category at Chanticleer International Book Awards.

Recently released is a two-book series—*How the West Was Won and Lost*. Book one, *Decimation*, is about the over-trapping of the beaver in the mid-1850s. The second book, *Annihilation*, is about the slaughter of the American buffalo in the same time period.

His picture book, *Charlie Lou Goes to the Rodeo*, was inspired by his granddaughter, Charlie Lou. Mr. Fleischauer hopes that this book will create awareness about autism.

Mr. Fleischauer has also published a book of short stories entitled *Just Another Morning*. It is a collection of shorts about US holidays and/or special events. The short story and title of the collection, *Just Another Morning*, is about September 11, 2001 and the tragic events on that day. September 11 was, in fact, just another morning ... until it wasn't. It was a semi-finalist in the Short Story Contest.

Alan was also awarded first prize in the 2020 Poetry Contest sponsored by Two Sisters Publishing. *Suicide Is Forever* is the title of the poem. Additionally, his short story, *42 Cents*, was a first-place winner with Two Sisters.

All of Mr. Fleischauer's novels are available on Amazon.com and through his website: Ealanfleischauer.com

Alan lives in Victoria, Minnesota with the love of his life—his wife, Paula.

Made in the USA
Middletown, DE
16 September 2024